AMIDST THE STONES OF FIRE

Amidst the Stones of Fire
by William Siems

ISBN: 978-0-09997026-4-2
eISBN: 978-0-9997026-8-0

First printing - December 2017

Scripture quotations from the SUV (Siems Unauthorized Version) of the Bible

Contact the author at siemsrj@live.com

Cover by Jacob Bridgman

Interior design by Alane Pearce, Professional Writing Services LLC MyPublishingCoach.com.

Dedication

This novel would not exist without the hard work, dedication, persistence, and encouragement of a lot of folks; especially my wife (Nancy), my kids (especially Angela), my grandkids, and a group of friends (of special note are Keith Timmer and Stephanie Dupea) who kept saying, "You should publish this," or "When will I get to read the (whole) book?" and specifically one pastor (among many), Tom Isenhart, who believed in me and called me into this part of my destiny ("He thinks I have a team.") and the the Liberator (Jesus) that we both follow.

LISA- I HOPE MY BOOK (YOU'LL HAVE TO PURCHASE THE SEQUEL) WILL PROVIDE SOME FUN IN THE MIDDLE OF THE OTHER TWO.

BLESSINGS
BILL SIEMS
SEPT 2019

Table of Contents

Preface

Back in 1948 the creation of the sovereign State of Israel rocked the Christian world. It rocked again when Israel miraculously won the Six Day war in 1967. Some said both of these events marked the beginning of the end times and the soon return of Jesus (the Liberator). Then came the publication, in 1970, of the runaway best seller "The Late Great Planet Earth" by Hal Lindsey and the rise of all manner of "End Times" and prophetic conferences. During the early 70's, in the middle of the Jesus People movement, the seeds for this book were sown. While it has taken over forty-five years to complete, it has continued to percolate in the back of my mind and heart. Many people dream and/or desire to write a book. Some say that we all have a book hiding inside of us, but few of us ever let it see the light of day. In these last few years this novel has often reared its lovely head and whispered, "Finish me, finish me." With a concerted effort over the last six months, I have.

This novel is an apocalyptic fantasy, a work of fiction. Any relationship of its' characters to real people or events is simply coincidence. Some will try to attack its theology. I would simply remind them that this is not a book on theology it is only a novel.

William Siems
Christmas 2017

Note: After the first chapter, the following chapter will begin with an epigraph (a short pithy saying from somewhere or someone) and a copy of the Stone-Star graph that will have been updated to include the stones and the people they have been entrusted to up to that point. I hope this will facilitate your ability to keep track of them all.

PS- There is also a "Glossary of Names as Introduced" at the end of the book.

Prologue

Hung around the neck of the prophet was the Urim. Hung around the neck of the priest was the Thummim. The two of them were encircled by the following; Logan, Piper, Jon, and Bahn, Zemir, Dal, Tanahiel, and Todah, Julius, Anna, Adam, and Meshar. The prophet held his staff aloft and spoke with a voice as clear as crystal. "Take off your shoes. This ground is about to become exceedingly holy and I want you to feel the full impact of it." Those who could complied. He continued, "Take out the stone that each of you possesses and hold it forth." Each of the twelve removed their stone from its resting place and held it out before them. "It is now the privilege of each of you, as individuals, to choose to relinquish your stone."

The Stones of Fire

PART 1

ORIGINS

Chapter 1- In the Beginning

Some things we know about the beginning. Like "God said Let there be light and there was light." but there are a lot of details we don't know.

from the "Musings of an old Pastor"

Chapter 1- In the Beginning

In the beginning, God made a garden. It was an incredible place. Everything and everyone cooperated with everything and everyone else. Things grew for the shear pleasure of it. There was no blight, only beauty and a virtually intoxicating fragrance. It was a place full of light, color and unbelievable music. There was a gardener assigned to the garden. His name was Ha-Geen (short for Ha-Geenithon, but no one had called him that since time immeasurable). Everyone loved him, responded to him, enjoyed his presence, and followed his desires and wishes. As he walked through the garden singing, it was as though the Lord of the garden Himself was there breathing life into all things, yet Ha-Geen was a cripple. He had been damaged in the war. When the choirmaster revolted and a third of the stars were darkened, Ha-Geen had been injured and, for some reason, left that way. Now he cared for the garden and prepared it for the return of the man and his bride. Since the fall of man and woman, the garden had been rendered inaccessible to them, but a longing for it remained in their hearts until the day they would be permitted to return, in the fullness of time. Until then, Ha-Geen tended the garden and the cherubs obscured the pathway to it with illusion and power.

In the center of the garden an underground spring bubbled forth into a large pool just shy of being a lake. In the middle of the pool grew a large tree whose branches reached to the sky. The Tree was called Chayeem, which is translated… Ha…..Ha….(many breaths)….Ha, ha, ha (laughter). Ha-Geen walked naked among all of creation for man had taken shame with him when he left the garden.

One day, as Ha-Geen was walking through the garden singing, he stumbled. He seemed to be doing a lot of that recently. Retracing his steps to discover what he had stumbled upon, he was surprised to find a large stone, as large as his fist and black as night. Removing his sword, he picked it up and struck the stone with the sword's hilt, producing a deep resonating dummmmmm that spoke of doom. A coldness seemed to envelop him and he puzzled. Hmmmm, what should he do with the stumbling stone dummmmm? At that moment his friend Zebo appeared, bounding out of a nearby thicket.

Zebo asked, "What have you got there Ha-Geen?"

"I'm not sure," he responded.

"Where did it come from?" asked Zebo sniffing the stone, and Ha-Geen showed him the place where he had stumbled.

"What will you do with it?" questioned Zebo.

"Of that I'm not sure either," said Ha-Geen. "Would you take me to the pool of Selah?"

"Certainly," said Zebo, "climb aboard."

So Ha-Geen mounted Zebo, and together they made their way to the pool of Selah. There, in the meadow on the shore of the pool, they stopped and Ha-Geen called all of the animals. (Tarzan yell, "Aheeahhhhhhh," well probably not like that).

Soon the meadow filled with all sizes and shapes and species. Ha-Geen held the doom stone aloft, singing, "Did anyone lose this?" A terrible stillness settled over the assembly. "Then I will go and ask of Chayeem," he sang. He stepped out upon the water and walked across the pool to the great tree.

Reverently addressing the Tree, he sang, "Chayeem, I stumbled upon this along my way today. What is it and what should I do with it?"

"Ah," intoned Chayeem, almost discordantly, as he looked upon the stone. "It is a wrong left here by the dark one when he slithered out of the garden after the fall of man. Hold it forth, Ha-Geen, and I will take care of it."

Ha-Geen held the stone in front of himself and one of the branches of the Tree positioned itself above the stone.

"Ha-Geen, draw your sword and chop off the branch in front of you!"

Reluctantly Ha-Geen drew his sword. "You.....want me.....to.... chop off this branch?" he asked.

"Yes!" replied Chayeem.

Never, in all the time that Ha-Geen could remember, had anyone harmed the Tree Chayeem. He couldn't bring himself to do it.

"It's OK, Ha-Geen, trust me." encouraged Chayeem.

Ha-Geen closed his eyes, held his breath, and chopped off the branch. A pain he had never felt before engulfed his soul and tears welled up in his eyes. Time stood still, the sword slipping from his hand. He wanted to cry out, but the anguish was beyond words. As a tear trickled down his cheek, he slowly opened his eyes. He saw a drop of sap fall from the wounded branch onto the black stone. The stone began to change, reduce in size, not shriveling up, but compressing until it was the size of a walnut, its color fading shifting from black, to smokey gray, to clear as crystal. Time began again.

Chayeem spoke, "This is the Urim, the Stone of Lights that adorned the breast of the luminescent one, before he was darkened. Please, place it next to the Stone of Truths, the Thummim." The heart of the Tree opened to display the Stone of Truths and an empty place for the Stone of Lights. "One day, these two stones will be gifted to the sons of men, but for now we will keep them here, safe."

Ha-Geen placed the stone, which was now full of light and beauty and warmth, into the socket that was prepared for it, and the opening in the heart of the Tree closed up.

"Thank you, Ha-Geen, for bringing me the stone," sang Chayeen. "Harmony and balance have once again been restored. You are much more than a gardener, Ha-Geen, but for now be content."

"I am, my lord," responded Ha-Geen.

"Yes, you are!" boomed Chayeem, "Yes, you are!" His laughter filled the garden, and all of the animals joined in.

Many years have passed, but the garden has not changed noticeably. The years have rested lightly on Ha-Geen and his friends. Chayeem has announced the return of the man, and anticipation is high. At the appointed time all are gathered at the meadow, facing the pool and its wondrous tree. The animals wait in rest and silence, and Ha-Geen and all who can kneel are kneeling. Suddenly the opening of a portal between the realms obscures the Tree and the man steps through to stand before them. In a voice both deep and melodious he announces, "Behold, I make all things new!" He reaches down, touches Ha-Geen and restores his injured wings. All of creation responds in thunderous worship and then becomes still again as the man raises his pierced hands.

"Thank you for tending and guarding this place for me. Prepare it now to receive my bride for I go to fetch her, and in a little while I will return."

All of creation responds, "Yes, my Lord!"

The man steps back through the portal and it closes.

Ha-Geen turns to the animals, stretches his wings, and says, "It will soon be very good once again," and launches himself into the sky.

Chapter 2 - Before the Beginning

"...between Genesis 1:1 and Genesis 1:2 of the Bible there was a cataclysmic judgment ... pronounced upon the earth ... as the result of the fall of Lucifer (Satan) and the ensuing verses of Genesis chapter 1 describe a re-creation or reforming of the earth from a chaotic state and were not an initial, but a secondary creative effort on the part of God."

from J. C. Scofield's the "Gap Theory of Genesis Chapter One"

You were the covering archangel appointed to guard everything. I placed you on My holy mountain. You walked in the midst of the stones of fire. You were completely perfect from the day you were created until... Ezekiel 28:14-15b

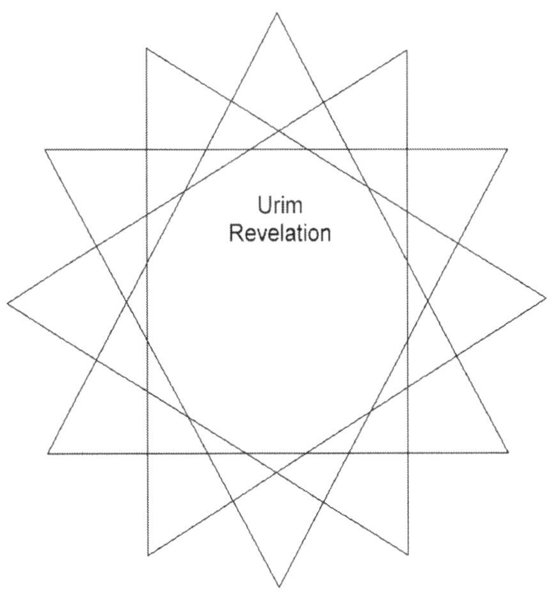

Before the beginning, there was a garden. In the middle of the garden grew an orchard, and in the middle of the orchard two wooden pillars reached to the heavens. They seemed to be twins yet a pillar of cloud engulfed one and a pillar of fire the other. A portal hovered between heaven and the garden, and angels walked in the garden and sometimes perched in the larger trees to rest from flying. Twelve luminescent stones surrounded the pillars. Perhaps the stones reflected the light or gave off a light of their own, but they appeared to be the colors of ruby, topaz, and diamond; of peridot, onyx, and amber; of sapphire, aquamarine, and emerald; of amethyst, garnet, and zircon; and two other stones beyond description.

Between the two pillars and amidst the stones of fire dwelt an angel of indescribable beauty. His entire body seemed to be covered with an intricate pattern of golden pipes and sockets, surrounding every manner of precious stones. His every breath created a symphony of unimaginably beautiful music with lights flashing in unison with it. Sometimes the music and the brilliance of the lights rivaled that of the sun itself, overshadowing everything that there was and all that it seemed there ever could be. The angels would join him to form a choir of praise that it was by his nature to produce and perform. He was the choir director, choreographer, and conductor of worship and his name was simply Hal.

One day, as God walked in the midst of the garden, He stopped in front of the two pillars, as was often His custom, and listened to Hal's latest symphony. At a pause in the music,

He informed Hal, "I have decided to create another race of beings. I will create a race in my own image and likeness. Let me show you a vision of what I intend so that you may compose a symphony worthy of them, my finest creation."

The Lord showed Hal His plan. Hal bowed deeply before the Lord, and the Lord left the garden.

Hal, however, was deeply troubled. He had thought that he was the crowning achievement of God's creative genius. He doubted that there could be anyone or anything more beautiful or more wonderful than himself, and for the first time in his life he doubted the wisdom of God. He reached down and gripped the pipes that surrounded his heart. He gripped them so hard that he actually distorted them, twisted them. Discord suddenly entered his compositions. It opened up entirely new realms of music and expression to him. He felt it was better, much better. Many of the angels quit listening to his music. It seemed less like worship and more like a performance. But about a third of the angels remained, entranced by this new thing. They had never heard anything like it. It stirred them deeply, and they found themselves agreeing with it at an elemental level. At some point Hal's lyrics began to express the new topics of his heart; doubt, error, and finally revolt.

Why did the Lord do nothing? Did He not know, could He not see the outcome? Of course He could, but He could also see the potential for greater good that even these things might contain. So the Lord let this discontent ferment until it finally resulted in open rebellion and war. Hal and his followers were thrown out of heaven, and God translated the garden to its new resting place. He called it earth, and the two pillars became two trees. With Hal's rebellion, the pillar of cloud appeared as a tree of the knowledge of good and evil, while the pillar of fire purified itself into a tree pulsating with the life of God Himself. The portal between heaven and the garden remained opened. Then

God completed His plan to create man. Man was wondrous to behold. He looked like God, inside and out. God placed man in the garden to guard it and to work with it, that it might produce to its fullest. Everything cooperated with man, and it was good. God called the man Clay. God told Clay that he could eat of the produce of any of the trees in the garden with the exception of the Tree of the knowledge of good and evil. That tree had been tainted by Hal's rebellion.

One morning, as God and Clay were sitting on the bank of the garden's river which was often their custom, God said, "Clay, it is not good for you to be alone. I am going to make someone to come along side you and be your helper." So God fashioned out of the ground the beasts of the fields and the birds of the air and brought them to Clay. Whatever Clay would call them, that became their name, yet He deemed none of them worthy to come along side of man as his equal, his partner, his helper.

So God put Clay to sleep and while he was asleep, God formed woman from that which was closest to man's heart, his rib. And when God was through with this, the crowning achievement of all of His creation, He woke Clay and presented woman to him. Clay's reaction can hardly be put into words. This was not some "other" that God had created to help him. This was the rest of God that until now he had not even dreamed existed. This was all that God was and that Clay was not yet. This was the beginning of all things "very good." And he called her Dawn for she was the start of everything new and fresh, and he embraced his wife and felt whole and complete.

One morning, as Dawn walked through the garden assembling breakfast from the produce of all of the trees, she came upon the Tree of the knowledge of good and evil that stood in the middle of the garden and found an angel of indescribable beauty perched in its branches. She stopped, transfixed by his beauty. The angel spoke, and when he spoke, it took her breath away. Here were sounds the likes of which she had never before heard. Then she realized that he had not yet spoken, but was only breathing.

When Hal saw Dawn, he too was awestruck and realized that if anyone or anything could be more beautiful than himself, this was she. He gasped in utter amazement. His gasp produced intensely captivating music. He determined that he had to have this woman for himself. As he exhaled, something stirred within them both, something primal that Dawn had never felt. It might have been the beginning of lust, but there was no wickedness in Dawn's heart, yet.

Hal spoke and his words radiated light and music, "I see that you are gathering produce for your meal. Here, have one of these." And he offered her a fruit from the Tree.

Dawn replied, "We have been told that we are allowed to eat of every tree except this one. To even touch this fruit will bring about the end of all things as they are!"

Hal's laughter filled the air with something quite different than glee, "It will not be the end of things! God knows that eating this fruit will bring about the beginning of enlightenment. You will be as full of light as I. You will be as full of light as God Himself. That is why He has kept it from you."

Hal extended the fruit again. It seemed to glow with a light all of its own. As she looked at it, she felt the desire within become a raging fire. As she took it and nothing untoward happened, she realized it was the source of a light she had been denied. As she bit into it, she felt a passion rising in her heart towards Hal that made her blush. Suddenly, she realized that Clay stood next to her. She extended the fruit towards him, its pungent aroma extending to encapsulate him as its juices dripped to the garden floor.

Time seemed to stand still as Clay took in all that was happening around him. Now, he had a choice to make. The flush that enveloped Dawn because she had eaten the forbidden fruit called strongly to his soul that he should join her or lose her forever, but deep in his spirit he knew there was another option. God had said that eating of the fruit of the Tree of the knowledge of good and evil would bring about the end of all things, but might it not be possible for him to transcend that law with something even greater, something deeper, something more powerful? What if Clay took Dawn to God and offered his own life for her transgression? Could he fulfill the obligation of the law with the gift of his life? But then Dawn would be alone in the world. Who would protect her, who would take care of her? As Clay turned to face the angel Hal, he knew that he could not leave her to face an uncertain future alone. He chose to be with her and took the fruit and ate. And his eyes became enlightened, and he realized that they were naked, and he was ashamed. They picked fig leaves and covered their nakedness from the eyes of the angel. Dejectedly, they walked from the Tree. Later, they wove the fig leaves into aprons to cover their nakedness more permanently.

In the cool of the day they heard God walking among the trees of the garden, and they hid themselves.

God called to Clay, "Where are you?" and the man answered, "I heard You, but I was afraid to come to You because I am naked, so I hid."

God said, "Who told you that you were naked? Have you eaten of the Tree that I asked of you not to eat?"

And man replied, "The woman that you gave me, she offered me the fruit, and I ate."

And God said to the woman, "What have you done?" and the woman replied, "The angel tricked me into eating it."

God spoke to the angel, and the breath of His anger seemed a fire of intense degree, "Because you have done this you are cursed of all created things. No longer shall you fly or even walk, from now on you shall crawl upon your belly, eating the dust of the earth, and there will be war between you and the woman, between your offspring and hers. While you may bruise his heel, he will crush your head."

And the heat of God's anger melted the pipes and sockets of Hal's soul and fused them into plates like scale armor, and the angel fell to the ground and slowly, painfully, slithered out of the garden. As he crawled, two of the large jewels from his breastplate were dislodged and left along the path of his retreat.

God then turned to the woman and said, "I will greatly multiply your pain in childbirth. You will bring forth your children in pain. Your desire will be for your husband and he will rule over you."

God then addressed Clay, "Because you have listened to the voice of your wife rather than mine, and eaten of the Tree that I commanded you not to, the ground is cursed because of you. No longer will it cooperate with you, but you will toil to bring it into submission and receive thorns and thistles as your reward. No longer will you eat freely of the trees, but labor to grow plants from the field. Your bread will be the result of the sweat of your toil until you return to the ground from which you were taken. For you are dust and you will return to dust."

And God turned to the animals that had gathered to witness and spoke. "Who will cover man's guilt and shame?" Two lambs stepped forward and bowed before the Lord their God. Man and woman each laid their hand on the head of a lamb, and all of them walked back to the two trees in the middle of the garden. And the lambs laid down their lives for the man and the woman, and God made garments of their skins to clothe the man and the woman. Another angel, beautiful and fierce, ushered the man and the woman out of the garden and stood guard at its entrance with his twin, both of them holding flaming swords so that the way to the Tree of life was blocked and guarded. And the Tree of the knowledge of Good and Evil was uprooted and cast out of the garden, and the ground wept. It wept for the lambs that were slain. It wept for the loss of man's innocence. It wept for the violation of the garden. It wept until the Tree of life was surrounded by a pool of water, and the portal to heaven was closed and another gardener was left to tend the garden. And the Lord touched the carcasses of the two lambs and they were revived and made as though they had never died.

One day, much later, the pelican Kate was flying through the garden with her angelic friend Zemir (which is translated, song). Although they were so different, they had many things in common, wings being one of them, and they enjoyed each other's company immensely. They flew across the great pool in the midst of the garden, decided to stop for a short rest, and landed among branches of the great Tree, Chayeem, that grew in the midst of the pool. While all of the trees provided food for those who lived in the garden, it was the fruit of the great tree that provided the inner life that maintained the animals' and birds' ability to speak and understand each other and the angels. No one thought it strange that they all spoke and understood the same language. No one had ever known it to be any different.

Zemir, called away into action, left Kate alone on the branch. Looking out across the pool, her eye caught something in its shallows. A dark something that pulled at her in an unusual way. She left her perch and sailed to the water's edge. Standing there, she could still see the object as it pulsated a deep brown in about a cubit of water. She stepped into the water. The water around the stone seemed to pulsate also, colder, then warmer, then colder again. Reluctantly, she dipped her beak into the water and retrieved the object. It appeared to be a stone about the size of one of her own eggs. Holding it in her beak felt somewhat disorienting. What should she do with it now? After a few moments she took flight and landed back in one of Chayeem's lower branches. Chayeem was not only the great tree in the middle of the garden's pool, Chayeem was also the wisest person in the garden, so it was not by accident that Kate flew back to the Tree. Kate waited a moment to regain both her balance and bearings,

She asked Chayeem a question. "Chayeem, I have found something odd, could you help me with it?"

"Let me see what you have," spoke Chayeem in a voice the was both melodic and deep. Kate opened her bill to reveal the stone. Chayeem spoke again, "Hmmm, it is a great wrong, lost to the dark angel when he retreated from the wrath of God. Lay it in the leaves of my branches." Kate obeyed. "Now, please take one of my fruit and squeeze its juices onto the stone." Kate complied. As the juice hit the stone it hissed and sputtered, giving off a pungent smoke. When the chemical reaction ceased and the smoke cleared, what remained appeared to be a large sapphire, yet more than that, for it seemed to glow with its own light. Chayeem spoke again, "Yes, it is as I had hoped. Once corrupted by the dark angel, it was difficult to tell, but now it is clear. This is the Thummim, the Stone of Truths. Here, I have prepared a place for it." Chayeem's branches moved back to reveal the Tree's trunk and its heart opened to reveal two empty places. "Please place the Stone of Truths in its place, Kate."

So Kate took the gem in her bill in order to place it in the Tree, but having taken it, found it difficult to release, as suddenly everything seemed to take on greater beauty and clarity. All things made sense in a new and wonderful way. Regardless of her feelings and what seemed like intense new revelation, Kate reluctantly deposited the gem in its place in Chayeem's heart. With deep gratefulness, Chayeem responded, "Thank you Kate, I know how difficult that was for you to do. I am glad that I was able to trust you with the task. I will keep the gem here until it is joined by the other and then I will keep them both until they may be entrusted to mankind. Thank you again." And Kate smiled as only a pelican can. Shortly, Zemir returned from his assignment and the two friends flew off to share the stories of their adventures.

Chapter 3 - Chayeem's Seed

Before time there were many Stones of Power, each endued with a particular characteristic.

from the "Sacred Book of the Stars"

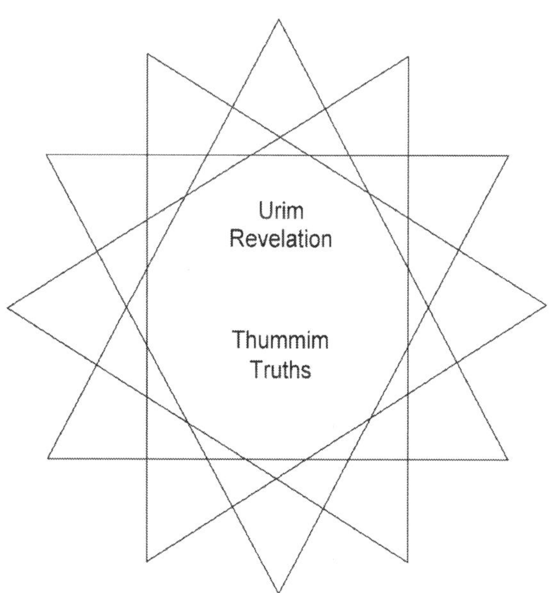

Zemir, the angel, flew about the garden, frolicking in its beauty, nearly intoxicated by the fragrance of the fruit of all of the trees and the flowers of the fields. He landed in the branches of the great tree Chayeem, temporarily exhausted from his flight. As he caught his breath, the presence of the Tree enveloped him, and he heard the words forming deep in his spirit,

"Zemir, I have a task for you, if you are willing," spoke the Tree.

"Certainly, my Lord!" Zemir replied.

"Take one of the fruit from my branches and cut it open with your sword."

Taking one of the fruit in his left hand, he removed his sword from it's sheath with his right, and sliced open the fruit to reveal a single large, brown seed.

"You may eat the fruit if you like, but I want you to take the seed to the Cherubim that guard the entrance to the garden," continued the Tree.

"And once I'm there?" questioned Zemir.

"They will let you know what you need to do next."

So Zemir ate the fruit. It was almost incapacitating. He wanted nothing but to stand there, balanced on the branch, and fully experience the joy and transplendent awe that it produced. Almost falling off the branch snapped him back to his senses and the task at hand. He flew the seed to the pool of Selah and washed himself and the seed.

He journeyed all the way to the eastern edge of the garden. There he found the two Cherubim who with their flaming swords guarded the entrance to the garden from the return of the man and woman. Zemir took one knee before them and holding the seed out before him.

He said, "Chayeem, the great tree, asked me to bring this, one of His seeds, to you."

Both of them also knelt in reverence to the seed. Together they reached out their flaming swords and touched it. Flames engulfed the seed and Zemir almost pulled back in reflex and dropped it, but he hesitated. The flame wasn't hot, it wasn't natural, it was supernatural. When the flame had completed its purpose, Zemir found the seed transformed into an emerald almost as large as his palm. It sparkled with a light all its own.

"Now," the angels said in chorus, «you may take the stone back to the great tree." Zemir closed his hand around the gem and prepared to launch himself into the sky, yet crouched a moment, immobile, wrapped again in the awe the stone produced in his hand. By sheer force of will he broke the spell and began his flight back to the Tree. Zemir landed in Chayeem's branches and held out the emerald.

He said, "Chayeem, here is the seed you gave me. It has been transformed by the cherubs into a jewel of awe."

"Yes!" said the Tree, "and where will we hide it until mankind is ready for it?"

"You are asking me?" responded Zemir.

"No, perhaps I was just talking to myself," the Tree chuckled. "Zemir , please take the stone to the pool of Selah and leave it there until it is needed," the Tree continued.

Zemir launched himself from the large branch on which he had stood, flew over the pool, and dropped the emerald into it. Kersplash! As it tumbled and weaved its way sparklingly towards the bottom of the pool, a large fish swallowed it, Galump!

Chapter 4 - The Lost Sword

To Wisdom, she is my friend. Make your ear attentive to her and incline your heart to her understanding; call out for insight and raise your voice. Seek her like silver and search for her as for hidden treasures, then you will understand the awe of the Lord and find the knowledge normally reserved for the Elohim.

from the "Book of the Proverbs"

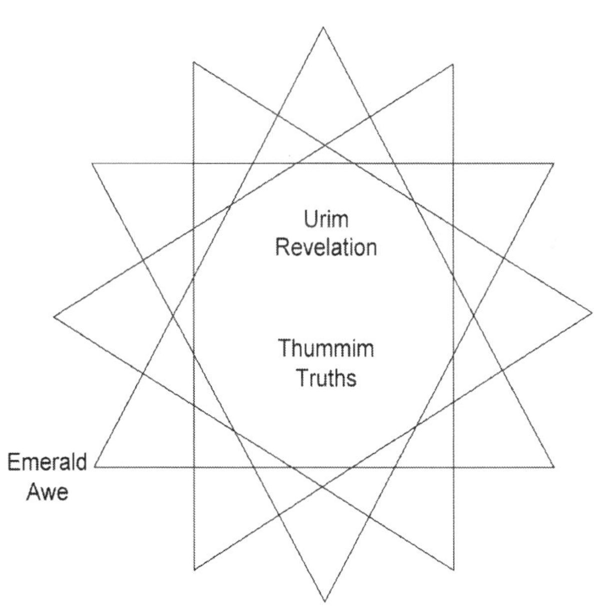

Before the foundations of the Earth were laid, when the morning stars sang together, and the sons of God shouted for joy, seven singing swords were given to the sons of Kaseel, the sons of Hope, or Foolishness, depending on your translator. But during the rebellion of the Choirmaster, two of the swords fell with the Nephilim, four remained with the angels. One was lost. This sword became know as Hail'yk, the wanderer. It had been entrusted to R'gel, the sixth archangel, but he died in the war of the Rebellion and his sword disappeared. Some say the Choirmaster shattered it with a note of utmost purity, but that tale is un-substantiated in the "Chronicles of the Elohim."

There are many legends concerning Hail'yk, its adventures, its lineage, but they are simply that: legends. No one knew anything for certain, until now.

Some Centaurs live for a very long time, others seem as immortal as the angels. Truth be told, they may all be killed, yet even then they do not perish. No one still living among men knew of a time before Alathos. It seemed that he had always been. In that way, he matched his friend, Melchizedek, the king of Salem.

Alathos lived in the garden with man and he left shortly after man. He took with him a bundle of herbs, spices, seeds, and a small troop of animals, an apprentice gardener, and some angels. Man went east and began to wander, while Alathos and his company turned north into the forests. They journeyed with more purpose than man, for the Tree, Chayeem, had shown

Alathos and the angels their destination. In the middle of the forest, they came upon a large meadow with a small spring fed pool. The entire place smelled distinctly of home and there they stayed.

That summer they built the few stone shelters they would need, planted the beginnings of the garden and laid the foundations for the pavilion and the smithy. In the middle of the pavilion, Alathos planted his herb garden and the single seed from the great tree Chayeem. Over the next few years everything flourished. The gardens grew, as did the Tree, the son of Chayeem. They even finished the pavilion with its circle of stones. Alathos finally had time for his hobby: working in stone, metal, and precious gems. Mazelot became a place of sanctuary and refuge.

Next to the pool Alathos finally enshrined his first statue of this the second age: a tribute to the archangel R'gel who had died in the rebellion. He left the wings off the statue, for the enemy had stripped them from him before he killed him, slowly. To a casual observer he might have looked like a mortal man, except Alathos had captured his regal bearing. The statue seemed almost lit from within because of the gems that he had used for his eyes. One gem Alathos had brought with him from the Lord's garden, The tree Chayeem had gifted it into his safekeeping. It was a large sapphire looking stone. The other was of an olive green peridot of uncertain origin. Where it came from Alathos never said. While seemingly strange, those that knew R'gel said the gems accurately reflected the different colors of his eyes, one blue and one green.

Late one evening the angel Zemir called Alathos and Bigtha, his apprentice gardener, outside to observe a spectacular meteor shower in progress. When it seemed over, Zemir and Alathos returned inside, but Bigtha remained outside in the fabulous night air. Suddenly another fiery orb lit up the sky, crashing down somewhere nearby in the surrounding forest. The shock and sound of it striking the earth reverberated so greatly that it knocked Bigtha to the ground as she screamed in alarm. Zemir and Alathos came running out of the house to her aid. As she got back to her feet, she pointed in the direction that it had fallen. The fragrance of its passing still clung to the air an uncharacteristically beautiful aroma, like a strongly-scented candle. Zemir launched himself into the sky to obtain a better vantage point of the crash site. Alathos invited Bigtha onto his back and they followed the directions Zemir called out from the sky. At the bottom of a large smoking crater, they found the fallen star split in two, exposing two veins of molten ore. They quickly returned to Alathos' smithy for two containers in which to harvest the ore.

The following day, Alathos heated his furnace hotter than it had ever been heated until the two containers vaporized exposing the veins of the raw ore once again. When they were pliable enough, Alathos fashioned them into two rods, twisted them together, and beat them mercilessly. He found to his amazement there was just enough material for two of the swords favored by angels and centaurs. So he cut the material into two lengths and proceeded to forge the first sword. He fired it, twisted it, beat it, and quenched it. Then he repeated the process again and again and again until satisfied with the blade. He then took up the other length and repeated the process, until again satisfied. He puzzled that during the process of beating each of the blades, they had not clanged as metal normally would. Rather, the tones they produced when beaten were strangely melodic, haunting yet beautiful. He honed them to a perfect edge and polished them to mirror brilliance. In the morning he would concentrate on their hilts. That night his dreams were also hauntingly strange yet beautiful. That next morning Bigtha awoke him at dawn and informed him that the Tree sought his attendance. As the son of Chayeem no one thought it odd that the Tree spoke. Alathos accompanied Bigtha to the herb garden with the short white tree in its midst. It had only grown to the height of a man, not nearly as imposing as the great tree Chayeem that lived in the center of the Lord's garden. It seemed when you were talking to the son of Chayeem, that you were talking more as equals, although that was hardly so. Being a centaur, Alathos was somewhat taller than the Tree, so in its presence he knelt.

With an unnecessary introduction, Bigtha began, "I have brought Alathos as you requested."

Keeping his head bowed in reverence, Alathos spoke, "You wished to see me?"

"Yes," responded the Tree. "I have a rather difficult request for you."

"You have but to ask," said Alathos.

"I know how much you treasure the two stones you placed in the eyes of the statue honoring R'gel, the sapphire my Father gave you and the peridot that you found along the way." He chuckled when he mentioned the peridot, knowing of its mystery. "I would like you to remove them from the statue and encase them on the pommels of the two swords you have just forged." Without an apparent breath the Tree went on. "You see, the ore that you found contains the last remnant of Hail'yk. So it would be only fitting that the two swords also contain R'gel's eyes. Wouldn't you agree?"

When Alathos finally caught his own breath, he whispered, "Yes, that would most certainly be fitting."

And so he did. He fashioned the hilts for the two swords that included pommels which contained the stones. The sapphire for the first two-handed sword which he named Sheecha-HaShamayeem, "the bringer of the heavens," and the peridot for the other sword which he named Nucha-Meshar, "to rest in peace."

Thus the wanderer Hail'yk finally came home to birth two additional singing swords, the HaShamayeem and the Meshar. Alathos lent the HaShamayeem to the angel Zemir and the Meshar he lent to Bigtha the gardener. Zemir took naturally to swordplay, being an angel, but Bigtha did not. So Alathos trained the two of them until Bigtha and Zemir together learned both the dance and the harmony of the two swords, until their sparring became something both beautiful to hear and a wonder to behold.

PART 2

TOWARDS THE CIRCUS

Chapter 5 - The Hunt

Each story has a beginning, a middle, and an ending, but life is not necessarily that orderly.

from the "Sayings of Pastor Jon"

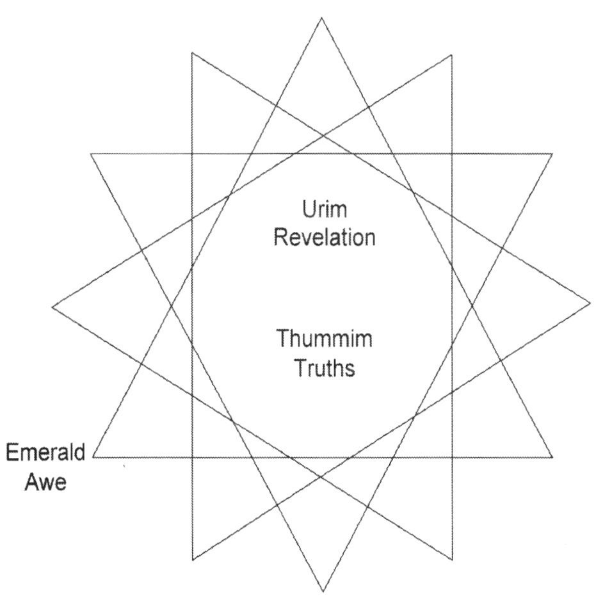

Dawn outlined the sky in a faint orange. Jon hoped that this of all mornings would be perfect. Sleep's icy fingers continued to cling to his thawing mind as he rolled over, hastily dressed against the chill of the morning, and crawled out of the makeshift shelter that had been the only substantial barrier between them and the elements. He hadn't heard Bahn leave the camp. His movements were far too quiet for recognition. Perhaps, after all of these months Jon's internal alarm clock still did not functioning properly.

He felt a mixture of indignation and disgust as he had awoken to the snap and crackle of an already smoldering campfire. Jon had forgotten to collect the wood last night before he had fallen asleep of sheer exhaustion. Today promised to, finally, be his complete initiation. Jon's heart, even now, was beating more rapidly with the anticipation of the day's events. However, he quieted himself and knelt by the fire. Why did he always seem to awaken late? Why, even on this morning? A sense of futility attempted to enter his mind. Would he ever be able to function as a woodsman and hunter? Some would say you needed to be born with those instincts, that some things just couldn't be learned. He shook his head to dispel these thoughts. The night had been clear and crisp, but a heavy dew covered the ground. The stars began to lose their brilliant sparkle, and he knew that Bahn would soon return. Still kneeling, he spoke almost imperceptibly, "Father, this is your day. I give it back to you. I give you myself, all of me.

Guide and direct me today. I wait for you." Falling silent he raised his eyes to the fading stars and waited. After a few moments the pressures of time and a life whose business sometimes suffocated him lifted off of his chest. A sense built, an awareness of that "presence" that he was beginning to know so well. Some would say he was just experiencing a simple state of mind following the quieting of his emotions. He knew otherwise. The peace came from an external source and was not a product of his own mind or imagination.

Noiselessly, Bahn emerged out of the thicket with a small armload of wood. Because of the morning dew the wood would be wet, and that would delay things even more. Jon wished he could call off the whole thing. The odds stacked themselves up against them. Bahn's single eye somehow spoke to Jon of hope. Bahn seemed to accept him as he was and felt that his progress was sufficient. He walked without hesitancy, with only the faintest hint of a limp that remained from the tragic accident that took the vision from his eye, leaving a mark of scars and an ancient name, Bahn. It was the word for "fire" in the ancient dialect of his people. The tragic fire that swept through the camp when he was young, killing so many of his people, had been catastrophic enough to give him a name. He and his grandfather had been among the few survivors. His grandfather had only lived a few days, regaining consciousness long enough to be told the extent of the damage. The hospital personnel had continually asked the old man what the young child's name was. His only reply was a far away look and the word Bahn, repeated over and over again. Bahn had been raised by a young missionary and his wife who had not simply taken pity on him but had genuinely loved the boy. He had always been a quiet and introverted boy who seemed to have a wonderful way with animals. He spent his mornings in the mission school, his afternoons working in the missionary's large garden, and all of his spare time in the dense woods of the surrounding countryside. He had remained with them for almost 20 years before Bahn told them late one night that he must leave.

Bahn smiled, an infrequent occurrence. It seemed as though he stood on the other side of today looking back at the events soon to take place. Or perhaps he was just pleased with his ability to find dry wood, when it all should have been wet with dew. They banked the fire together with the rapid precision of many months under Bahn's tutelage, their morning taking the shape of a well-practiced ritual. Into the boiling water Bahn placed the ingredients of what would shortly become a type of mush. It contained berries, nuts and an assortment of herbs and grains, all native to the area, most of which Jon, too, could find among the wilds, but about whose nutritional quality he knew little or nothing. Besides the mush Bahn prepared a hot herb tea sweetened with honey. Jon didn't know where Bahn found the honey. After breakfast, which never seemed to satisfy Jon's hunger but always provided him with enough energy for the morning, he grabbed his soap, towel, and a clean set of clothes from his knapsack which hung casually, almost carelessly, from one of the surrounding trees. What did Bahn call these trees? Sometimes it just seemed too much to remember. But Bahn continued to drill into Jon's mind, at least by his example, that little by little this must all become instinctive.

The morning ritual of bathing attempted to merge Jon further with nature, to make him less of an intruder and more of a human animal. As far back as Jon could remember, he loved to bathe, especially in the mornings, but this differed. How cold and lonely it could be in the morning, and yet his eyes beheld a remarkable beauty. The coldness gave way to an invigorating crispness. The loneliness turned into a silence which caused him to again perceive the "presence" neither animal nor human.

They traversed the single pathway to the lake more by touch than sight. The way led to a small natural beach. He wondered if Bahn brought this sand in by helicopter. The thought delighted him, the longer he dwelt on it. Bahn and a technological society differed more than night and day. An old gnarled stump of a tree reached its spider-like fingers into the lake. Jon laid his clean clothes on it and began to disrobe. With his soap and towel in hand, he entered the small lake as noiselessly as possible. They bathed every morning, less out of desire for cleanliness than a desire to identify with the woods, to be like another tree. That would be what Bahn would say. The water wasn't just invigorating it was jolly well cold today. He waded into the water knee-deep. The morning's full moon reflected in the silent crystal waters. He lathered up from the waist down, then waded deeper into the water. Ah...Well, that was the worst of it, cold enough to freeze your socks off. He lathered up chest, arms, face and hair. The fragrance, that was the funny part. There was no fragrance, and yet you were sure you smelled something, maybe it was an absence of odor. Perhaps the soap removed the smells of the night and somehow left you empty and ready for the smells of the day. Bending over, he washed his face, soaped his short cropped hair, and then waded into the chest deep water. Just as he completely submerged himself, his mind jumped back to the day he was baptized.

Jon had always been a religious boy, but it wasn't until he was a young man at Bible School that he had been baptized. He had finally found the difference between a ritualistic religion and an actual relationship with God, and had asked to be baptized. He still remembered the feeling when he came out of the water. His face radiated, and he spoke fluently in what appeared to be a foreign language. Above all else he felt clean clear through, as though he had taken a bath on the inside.

A spirit of anticipation coursed through Jon as he rose out of the water. Today something of significance was going to occur. Then he saw them: two lights pulsating in the water nearer the shore, one was a light blue in color, the other a yellow brown, amber, maybe. He walked towards the amber one closer to him. Reaching down into about a cubit of water to find the source of light. He grasped a jewel nearly as large as his palm and strangely warm and almost collapsed into the water. A feeling of radiant life overwhelmed him. After a few moments the feeling subsided and he began to breathe normally again. Jon pointed out the blue light to Bahn who had nearly left the water and Bahn returned to recover a light blue aquamarine jewel. They quickly waded out, dried off, and began dressing. They stood for a moment comparing the stones. Jon shared with Bahn his experience of breathtaking life. Bahn said that as he had grasped his stone he had clearly heard the words, "Never give up!" deep in his spirit. They placed the stones in their packs and continued their morning ritual of taking pine needles from the nearby trees and rubbing them into their clothing. The fragrance of the pine, now assimilated by their clothing, would mask any of their human odor throughout the day. The equipment in their day packs consisted only of a light lunch and a few other necessary items. They both strung their hunting bows, and Jon attached an arrow holder to his. Jon continued to use the shorter hunting bow to which he had grown accustomed. Bahn used a bow that he himself had made, shaped more along the lines of a long bow than Jon's shorter one with its curved limbs. Bahn used no bow quiver, but simply carried three extra arrows clasped in the hand in which he held the bow. Jon's bow, being of a more recent design and manufacture, shot quicker than Bahn's and with more striking power. But what Bahn lacked in the quality of his equipment, he made up for in his personal hunting ability.

They headed silently for the rise. Walking a few yards apart through the sparse brush. Bahn navigated the woods by simple instinct, as though he were a part of them. Jon, on the other hand, had to concentrate heavily on stepping in the right places so as to make the least amount of sound. The early morning dew which shrouded the entire landscape clung heavily to them as they continued to make their way toward the four alpine lakes which for the past months had become their daily tramping ground. They skirted the first and second lakes, which still lay silent in the growing morning light. The wind this morning was truly in their favor, blowing lazily towards them. They made their way to the next and larger of the lakes, staying at least one hundred yards from its banks. At last, they were within sight of their destination, an inlet to this larger lake. There, near the deep pool that was fed by a glacial waterfall, they had often observed a small herd of deer coming each morning for water. Their primary goal was the leader of the pack, the king stag that led the entire herd. Having scouted this area for weeks they knew the herd's general habits. At sunrise the king stag would lead them away from the lake and over the ridge onto grazing land. They planned to wait, disguised on the ridge, for the herd to approach. However, this morning they were late. They were still a few minutes from the ridge when the sun broke over the neighboring peaks and shed its strong clear light down to the lake below.

Bahn continued to head for the ridge with his slow, steady stride. Jon aborted their original plan and attempted to cut across the ridge early to ambush the deer from the other side. As Jon reach the top of the range he stopped for a short breather. Strange that the wind which had been blowing in his favor coming up the ridge should continue to blow in his face on the other side, but it did just that. He had thought things would have to go according to their original plan in order for it to all work out, but today he was learning his greatest lesson about hunting. True hunting does not consist in setting up and executing the perfect trap, but in the skill that provides the hunter with the ability to improvise according to the needs of the day. He started down the other side of the ridge towards the grazing land when a majestic site stopped him cold. There, on the ridge line, stood the king stag. Jon recognize the large animal immediately, having seen him often during the past weeks. It was almost as if they knew one another. The stag strolled along the top of the ridge and then turned sharply to cut straight down towards the meadows below. Estimating the stag's present speed, Jon took a diagonal in order to cut across his path. A couple of does would soon follow the stag, but Jon was not interested in them. He wanted to intercept the stag on the other side of the large outcropping of rock. Jon had to hold a tight rein on himself now because of the excitement building up inside of him. He reached the edge of the outcropping ahead of the stag. At least, he thought so, for he saw no animals. Jon took one knee, his accustomed stance, and waited.

The wind picked up a little, bringing with it the chill of the morning, beginning to stir the treetops. The thrill of excitement rose in his breast accompanying the wind's chill. Jon shivered slightly and nocked the razor-sharp broadhead arrow to his bowstring. Then everything stopped. He heard the stag moving through the brush. He perspired heavily from the waiting, as badly as he had during the climb up the ridge. He couldn't see the deer well, only the outline of its form. It seemed smaller, but the brush obscured it. The deer stepped out into the open. Not the stag, a doe. Had the stag already passed? Jon got out of his kneeling position and began to move silently in the doe's direction. He moved quietly enough that the doe did not hear him The wind blew so that the doe could not smell him either. As long as she didn't turn around and see him he would be okay. He crept closer, his arrow still nocked and ready on the bowstring. Then something made him turn back towards the brush out of which the doe had come. Perhaps some movement or something he had heard, but he turned, and there stood the stag. Jon paused, awestruck. At this distance he seemed large enough to be an elk. His beautiful and symmetrical rack of his horns testified to his age and experience. This was truly going to be the final test of his initiation. He wished he were closer. He was afraid of spooking the great stag. The stag put his head down to eat something behind the bush and Jon moved stealthily ten yards closer. He knelt again and brought the bow into position. The king stag lifted his head and walked fully out into the clearing a scant thirty yards away. Jon slowly pulled back his arrow to its full draw length and sighted on the kill spot. Just before loosing his arrow, the sweat of strain beading on his forehead, he whispered a one word prayer in his head, "Father." With a nearly silent twang of the bowstring, the arrow launched. The stag, however, heard the bow and its majestically racked head instantly flinched in alert, its nose and ears keenly aware that something nearly imperceptible indicated danger, but it was too late. The arrow sped home, a little higher than he had wanted, but landing with a resounding slap just behind the shoulder.

In that first instant the stag seemed unaware of the arrow piercing its side. A quick turn of its head and it saw Jon. The stag turned fully and in savage fury attempted to charge, but his legs crumpled beneath him. Jon rushed to the side of the beast who now panted heavily. He looked into his large brown eyes as the stag attempted to lift its head. Suddenly a voice brought Jon back to reality. Though Bahn was nowhere to be seen, Jon distinctly heard him say "Kill him, he's suffering!" Jon dropped his bow and unsheathed his large hunting knife. Then, cradling the head almost lovingly, he plunged the knife into the stag's throat. As he sliced, he felt a chill run up his spine, and a voice somewhere in the trees said, "He died for you!" Jon looked in the direction of the trees, but all he saw was a large bird taking flight.

When Bahn finally joined him, blood covered him up to his elbows as he field dressed the stag. They labored quietly for some time before transporting the meat back to the camp. Fortunately, the trip back was mostly downhill or it would have taken too much of the day to complete. They arrived in good time, although quite tired. Only when they had finally returned and settled in did Bahn finally speak. "You have done well today, my son." Jon smiled, that was enough.

Bahn had always seemed more like a father to Jon than his actual father. His father's legalistic version of religion seemed oppressive. Bahn had and lived something more pure, more natural, more elemental, more real. He had a relationship with God and did not just follow of a bunch of rules, regulations, and ceremonies. Bahn had also introduced Jon to the circus. The beauty of nature seemed reflected in this group of performers and their helpers who lived without pretense or facades. Jon attended the circus as often as he could and soon knew most everyone's name and function. He became a regular and they so appreciated his encouraging words that one day the Ringmaster met him at the gate. "Jon, a number of my performers and employees have shared with me over these past few month the deep impact that you have in their lives."

He handed him an envelope. "This is a season pass. We welcome you here as often as you can make it."

Jon was more than surprised, he was flabbergasted. "Thank you sir, I am extremely grateful that I have been allowed to be of some small help. However, you need to know that I am gaining more from your people than the the small encouragement I am able to offer. You need to know that you have something very special here."

The Ringmaster smiled, "Yes, I do. It is an opportunity to bring fun, joy, hope, and a little awe back into their everyday life."

Shortly afterward that Ringmaster added to his offer the chance to have weekly meetings with his people, meetings for worship, prayer, and more.

Chapter 6 - Little Anna

In the early 1800's the circus was first described as "The Greatest Show on Earth!"

from the "Arkansas Herald"

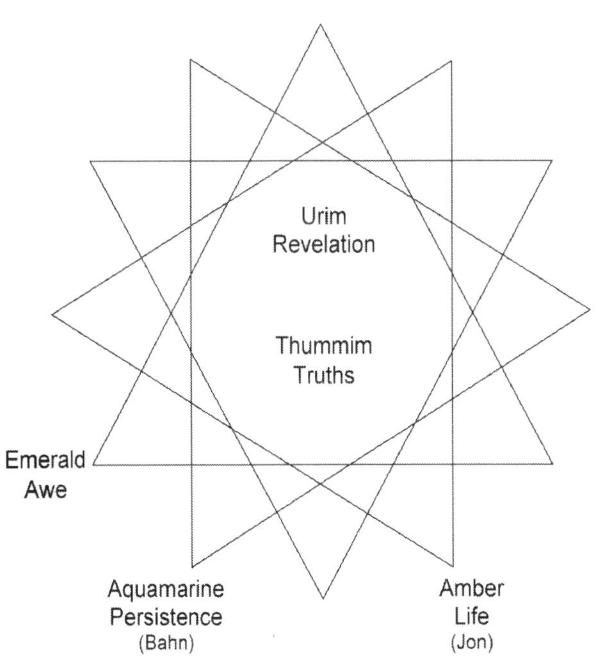

Young and pretty, she felt but a cinder child from a bad fairytale. Her father brooding darkly nary spoke a kind word to her. While claiming to follow the Lord of the Light, he more often served the Lord of Darkness. He made her life bitter. Her name, Anna, which means "moaning in travail" seemed appropriate. Her father was not an evil man, just an unsuspecting agent of the wrong spirit. While he thought he did right, he was doing the opposite. She tried very hard to please him, but try as she might she always fell short… somehow. She scored at the top of her class in school, but he made her feel silly and stupid. While only ten years old he expected her to do the work of an adult. The family owned a large garden and small orchard. Here she tried to find solace, at least when her father was absent, off on one of his adventures.

One particular day he gave her a small portion of the garden to weed. She determined that this time her performance would be flawless. It was nearly always so anyway. She worked long and hard, assuring that every weed and stray blade of grass had been removed. Finally, certain, she called her father to see what she had done. He inspected perfunctorily and tersely pronounced, "The garden looks OK, but you are impossibly slow." Hot tears trickled down her cheeks and as soon as he turned and left, she burst into devastated sobs that broke the heart of heaven.

On another day nothing seemed to go right and everything seemed to go wrong. While riding her bicycle on their private gravel road, her younger brother, father's favorite, threw a stick at her. It missed her, but caught in the spokes of her front tire, jamming it, stopping it immediately, and throwing her over the handle bars. She hit the gravel hard, flat out on her back, sliding a few feet down the road before coming to a stop. Struggling to breathe, she heard the screech of tires and painfully lifted her head to see her dog frozen in front of a speeding automobile. She quickly looked away and heard both the thump and the crunch. At that point she gladly gave up consciousness.

She awoke in her bed, painfully sore, her hands bandaged, her mother sitting beside her bed. Mother anchored her in the storms of her life, but could not make up for the devastation her father caused. An angel stood near her unseen nor acknowledged. Her guardian angel Zek. He often wished he could take more action on her behalf, but until now, the prayers that sustained him and the commands that moved him had not allowed him to do more. Hopefully, that would soon change.

The circus came annually to their small village, the highlight of each and every year as they always attended. For a few short hours she felt transported to another world. This year promised to be the best yet. She hoped to visit the circus on a school outing, as well as with her family. Since she completed the bulk of her chores early, her father allowed her to go on the school outing that would last past supper and the time when she normally would have been required to do her chores. Her family met her there for the evening performance.

They were sitting up high in the bleachers, on the edge of their seats, watching the high wire act. It was breathtaking, exciting, almost frightening. Suddenly someone began screaming. Every one turned to see what had happened. A fire had broken out in the food stand and was quickly spreading to engulf the entire big tent. Smoke and heat and more screams, and then nothing until she awoke in the hospital, burned quite badly. The doctors were surprised that she had survived. She had lost most all of her hair. It must have caught fire, for a bandage wrapped her entire head and covered her eyes so that she could not see. She could still hear, though, and she heard the doctors quietly talking to someone, the clown from the circus. Apparently he had rushed to her side, smothered the flames in his own costume, and saved her life. They said that with the severity of her burns, it would have almost been better if she had died, as she would never be able to see again. But she did not believe them. Every day the clown came to visit her, every day that the circus was in town. Each day they prayed together that somehow she would regain her sight. Without her sight, her hearing had improved dramatically, perhaps to make up for her loss. She now knew the footsteps of the clown. She could hear him coming from a long way down the hall.

Today, as he approached her hospital bed she said, “Hello Mr. Clown.”

“My, but your hearing is still improving,” he replied.

She smiled. Then she asked, “When did you get the scar behind your ear?”

Startled, he replied, “How do you know that I have a scar behind my ear?”

She laughed, “I saw it!”

Even more startled, he continued, “When did you see it?”

“As you were walking down the hallway to my room.”

And that was the first time that she shared with him that sometimes she could see, not with her eyes, but with her heart.

Chapter 7 - Julius

But we rejoice in our sufferings, knowing that suffering produces endurance, and endurance produces character, and character produces hope, and hope does not disappoint us.

Romans 5:3-5

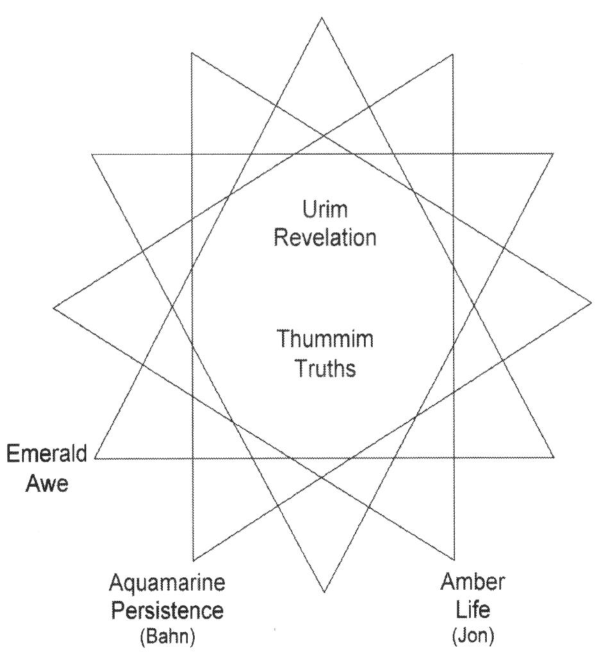

They named him Julius; that is, "youthful," after Julius Randle, the LA Lakers' basketball player in the early 21st Century, but his name actually meant "the Lord rolls like a thunder moving towards acting like a man." Although belittled for his name growing up, "Is your middle name Caesar? Julius Caesar? Hah, ha, ha!" his name truly called forth his destiny to become a man. He learned to roll with the punches, whether verbal or physical, and he learned to act like a young man, regardless. In sixth grade the class bully, Rex, was particularly brutal to Julius.

"Heh, Julie! How does it feel to have the name of a girl?"

Julius simply stood up to his full, short for a sixth grader, height and replied, "You have heard, 'Sticks and stones may break my bones, but names will never hurt me?' However, you need to know that the T-Rex dinosaur had a brain the size of a walnut."

Rex did not get it, but many of those around him did and they began laughing at Rex, which he could not stand. Rex hauled off and knocked Julius to the ground, bloodying his nose. That earned Rex a suspension from school and Julius a great deal of respect. He continued to use humor to help slough off those trying to wound his soul, never letting them crush his spirit. By high school he was a true humorist, not in the "cut-up" sense of the word, but because he always seemed to be able to come up with the right words or the turn of a phrase to put a smile on most faces. He verbally frustrated the bullies enough times that they finally let him alone and learned to respect him. Along the way he found the true value of humor: to open the human heart, to break up the dry ground of the spirit, and to prepare both for the simple implantation of hope, love, and truth.

He became entranced with magic tricks and sleight of hand. He never really wanted to become a full-fledged illusionist. He did incorporate many simple magic tricks like using cards, sponge balls, and whatever he could find into his humor. He loved working with younger kids and they loved him in return for both his humor and his magic tricks. He became a near legend at the children's hospital, where he would captivate the kids with his performances and, for a few short hours, take them far away from their troubles. It was then that he encountered the true magician, Maximist the Magnificent.

Maximist performed at the local circus and had for many years. He was also a very good judge of character. When Julius first visited the magic show, he impressed Maximist with by both his concentration and observation skills. Julius came up to chat with him after the performance and told Max the tricks he had figured out and also those he had not. He came back a number of times over the next few days until he understood all except two. Max invited Julius out to lunch, and their friendship blossomed for much more than the lad's simple love of magic and children. Maximist saw in Julius a character of greatness that surpassed his simple talent. He saw Julius' ability to touch the human heart.

Early one circus season, Julius showed up at the ticket counter only to find out that he had been granted a season pass. So, whenever he could get away from his other commitments, you would find him there, at the circus. Often he would get there early and, because he was now known to the performers and administration, they would let him in early. He would help Max set up his magic booth and sometimes even assist him in his shows. Every good magician needs a good assistant or two and Julius was such an addition that Max's shows grew and grew in popularity. Max began to try tricks he would never have been capable of doing with a lesser skilled assistant. When the performances would begin in the big top, Max would close down his booth and, after he and Julius had all the props safely stowed away, would share a trick or two with Julius.

"Julius," Max began, "A good magician is always in character, even when he is not performing. For instance, I knew an old Chinese magician who always walked bow-legged and with a waddle, so that when on the stage he could carry a large fishbowl between his legs as one of his props, and no one would notice." He continued, "and you should always be working to improve your execution! That reminds me," Max went on, "I would like to teach you a new card trick." Max then showed him a trick where using sleight of hand he moved a card, that Julius had previously selected, from the deck and held it horizontally within his palm between his second and third fingers. Then Max brought the side of his nearly closed hand down on the deck while simultaneously turning the card vertical with his thumb revealing the card while giving the illusion that the card had jumped from the deck and into Max's hand. They practiced it over and over and over again, until Julius mastered it. It didn't take long as he was a quick study!

"Max," Julius countered, when they seemed done with the card trick, "I have a story for you."

Max smiled slyly. "OK, but remember it's difficult to fool a magician," Max replied in turn.

"This story is about a magician," said Julius. "You see, this 75 year old gentleman and his 75 year old wife were on an airplane to Hawaii for their 50th wedding anniversary. She had the window seat and had fallen asleep, so he struck up a conversation with the nicely dressed younger man sitting next to him, only to find out he was a magician. "You're really a magician?" the older man asked. "Yes I am," said the younger man. "You don't look like a magician," said the older man. "Really, and what do magicians look like?" asked the younger man. "Oh, I don't know, I just would never have figured you for a magician. You really are?" "Yes I am!" he said as he smiled. "Let me prove it to you. I will grant you a wish." The old man's eyes grew big, "You will? What kind of a wish?" he asked. "Anything," said the magician. "Anything, really, anything!" exclaimed the old man. "Yup! Anything!" smiled the magician. The old man looked at his sleeping wife, then at the magician and back to his sleeping wife. He leaned over to the magician and whispered, "I wish my wife was 30 years younger than me." "Easy," said the magician. He said a magic word, and poof, the old man was 105!

Max burst out laughing, "Ha, ha, ha, I didn't see that one coming, that was GREAT! A hundred and five, that'll teach him. Be careful what you wish for."

Their relationship continued like this for a few years until, on one occasion when Julius showed up early, Max handed him an envelope. "Here, Julius, the Ringmaster gave me this. It's addressed to you." Julius pulled out his pocket knife and slit it carefully open. It contained a job offer, and so Julius began his own career with the circus, initially as an entertainer to those waiting in line to enter the big top. Julius had another amazing ability. He remembered names and faces. He would introduced himself to those waiting in line, carefully listen to them as they replied with their own name, ask them a couple of questions about themselves, and the next time they came to the circus he would greet them by their name. Wow! That made them feel special, and they were. Julius believed every person was special and unique. He continued to hone his personal and professional skills as a comedian and magician in front of the limited audience of those in line. He was so successful that it was soon evident he was much more than a line entertainer. Often times folks would be so engaged in his performance that they would hold up the line and people would crowd in front of them, but even that Julius handled with humor and tact. Finally, the big day came. The Ringmaster himself showed up while Julius was performing to his in-line crowd. He stuck an envelope in Julius' back pocket which Julius had to wait until later to open. The contents were an upgraded offer to be added to the performers in the big top as a member of the clown troupe.

His story of favor and success repeated itself again with the clown troupe. He began as a simple clown's apprentice, setting up props, acting as the object of their silly stunts, and capturing the hearts of the audience regardless. He would occasionally improvise or he would come up with some original material for the clowns to include, and they usually did, because his instincts and timing were uncanny. The rest of the troupe finally realized that they had no reason to fear that he would "steal the show." The times when he became the focus he would quickly turn the attention back to someone else. He was the consummate team player. Therefore, it was only natural that they allow him to script his own material as a lead clown, and he flourished in that role too. His intuition as to what would tickle the audience's fancy, and his utter humility, made him a joy to work with and a pleasure to follow. He would often pick someone out of the crowd and bring them into the ring to be part of his act. Here again, his choices showed flawless intuition. He never embarrassed a person, but always brought out the best in them, while greatly pleasing the crowd at the same time. It was with this gift, skill, or ability that he one day chose Anna, a young reclusive girl, to work with him in the ring. For Anna it was the highlight of her young life.

"For this next part of our act, we will need the assistance of a young person," he loudly proclaimed to the audience. A number of hands were instantly raised, but he had already noticed Anna for her concentration and silent participation up to that point. "Young lady, how about you?" he gestured towards her, where she was sitting with her family as he smiled. She looked around, pointed to herself and, when he nodded, she smiled and stood up. As she walked down from the bleachers and towards the ring, he shouted, "Let's welcome her into the ring!" and he began to applaud. The crowd followed suit. He held out his hand and she took it as he drew her to his side. "And your name?" he asked as he leaned down to her level.

"Anna," she replied bashfully.

"My friends, this is Anna." He said to the crowd and more applause followed. He had her stand on a small platform and slowly turned her around so all of the audience could see her, in her faded blue jeans and light pink blouse. He then gestured to two of his fellow clowns. They pulled out a large bed sheet, came to her, and proceeded to loosely wrap it around her. There was a flash of light like a fireworks explosion and then darkness. When the lights came back on, she stood there in a pink and white gown befitting a princess. "Never forget, you are as beautiful inside as you are now on the outside!" The crowd roared their approval. He took her hand and escorted her out of the ring, still in the gown, and she returned to her place with her parents, her countenance beaming.

"And now the incredible and daring high wire performance of Bruno and Natalia." he shouted as he pointed up to where they stood high in the air and he retreated to his chair in the wings.

That was the year that Maximus the Magnificent took ill. It started with what seemed like a winter's chill and a cold, but it never got better, only worse. Max was finally bed-ridden, hospitalized, and sent to the farm. The farm was owned by some friends of the circus, Jon and Mary, and there he was to live out his final days. Julius was his constant companion. Well, as constant as his busy schedule would allow. One day he arrived at the farm carrying a small box, a little larger than his fist. Max had instructed him to bring the box from among his things at the circus.

"In the back of my trailer, under a purple blanket with gilded edges, you will find an old trunk. Here is the key." The old man whispered, like a morning breeze. "In the bottom, under my magic books, you will find a small leather box. Bring it with you the next time you visit me," he had continued, finally running out of breath. He coughed hoarsely. Julius had found it, a simple dark brown leather box, tied up with a golden ribbon. He could tell that it was something special from the way Max had protected it, and with the near reverence with which he had described it. It was quite heavy for its size. He wondered desperately what it contained, but he did not open it. He just brought it with him on his next visit as Max had requested.

Max was resting, so Julius just sat at his bedside, the box on the end table, cradling Max's frail hand in his own. Max's eyes fluttered open. "Did you remember the box?" he softly whispered.

"Yes, sir, I did," Julius replied picking it up off the end table. Just seeing the box seemed to invigorate Max.

His eyes suddenly clear and sharp, he continued, "This has been passed down from father to son for generations until I received it from my father so many years ago." He stopped to catch his breath. "And while I have no son of my own, you are all the son I could have ever have hoped for." Tears formed in both of their eyes. "And so I give it to you. Please open it." A tear now coursing down his cheek, stunned to silence, Julius opened the box. It contained a large purple amethyst, that seemed to shine with a light of it's own. "This is the Hope stone, the stone of the King!" Max commanded with more strength in his voice than he had shown for weeks. "It is my only true magical possession." As Julius grasped the stone to remove it from the box, he realized Max's words were not just true, but a great truth. His entire being was overwhelmed with such a palpable presence of hope that it seemed to change everything. The air smelled of hope, he felt full of hope, and suddenly he believed that if he just said the words he could actually raise Maximus from his death bed. However, he blinked, and Max was gone. The light in his eyes had slipped away. As he began to speak the words that would raise Max from the dead, he heard Max's voice more clearly than ever say, "It's OK, Julius, I am not dead. I have only moved out of that old house. And remember, my son, how much I love you and how proud I am of you." Max was gone.

Chapter 8 - Logan

When you walk in the awe of God, it purifies and sustains you. If you desire to be wise, begin in awe and reverence for the Lord your God. Awe prepares the way for instruction and understanding. God is pleased with those who walk in the awe of His splendor and majesty.

from the "Seer's Words concerning Awe"

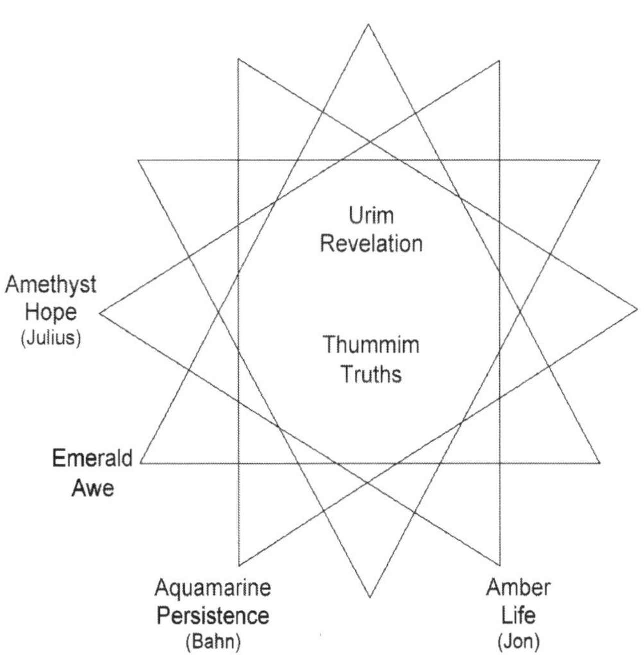

Born small although a full-term baby, Logan looked premature, fully formed but tiny. He matured slowly and, although he ate well, put on little weight. He proved slow to speak, slow to walk, slow to learn many things. Yet, he was fearless and determined, sometimes almost to the point of obstinacy. He had to be watched constantly and sometimes it was so tiring to do so. As he grew, even though he remained very short, a strange favor surrounded him, recognized and perceived subconsciously by both man and beast. Animals loved him: dogs, cats, horses, even the birds. It seemed as though he communicated with them on some level. People responded to him in a similar way. They often did not even know why, but they felt drawn to him simply, yet powerfully. It was amazing to see how much he loved and was loved by all.

Usually in school a dwarf would be pitied, looked down on, or ridiculed, but Logan experienced none of that. The special favor that he carried with him made him a friend to all. At sporting events he spent time with everyone: the athletes, the cheerleaders, the in-crowd, the outcasts, the nerds. To him they were all the same, special people. It made him the personification of school spirit as he brought all facets of the school, including the faculty, together as a unified whole.

Logan especially loved the circus. Each spring, all summer, and even into the fall, he constantly asked, "Can we go to the circus, can we, can we?" and often his family took him. While accepted at school, at the circus he seemed to have found his people. That is why when he turned 18, although not sure of his ability to make good, consequential decisions, it was no surprise that he left home with his parents reluctant blessing and joined the circus. The performers immediately accepted him with open arms and soon they wondered how they had ever gotten along without him. One day, when out fishing with the clown, he caught a large fish. When he unhooked it, it coughed up a huge emerald. He picked up the stone and was filled with awe. Suddenly he could hear all of the animals clearly, understand them perfectly, and they him. This, too, became evident to everyone at the circus, Logan had a special bond with all the animals. He gave them all names, often radically different from those their owner or the animal trainer had given them. The lion was no longer Leo, but Ariel. Queenie the lioness was amed Lebeah, the ape called Koph, the stallion was Kue, and the eagle Azenyah. It was only natural that Logan became the apprentice to the animal trainer. He fed the animals, tended them, cleaned up after them. He probably would have slept with them if it had been allowed. Horse whisperers accomplish nearly miraculous things with horses. Logan was an animal whisperer and without exception they all responded to his every wish.

The animal trainer, Jacob, and lion tamer, Aleshia, were reluctant to allow Logan into the ring during performances, afraid that he would steal their thunder or their applause, but he was welcome to wait in the wings and assert his special talents and abilities from there. That held true until the night a young child stumbled and fell into the ring. Aleshia was working the two lions. She had long ago dispensed with working with them inside of cages, as it definitely took the excitement and perceived danger to the next level to work with them in the open. The young girl screamed as she fell into the ring and then screamed again as the lion raced towards her. Aleshia unholstered the revolver that she wore, but before she could do anything else, Logan had stepped into the ring and commandingly shouted "Stop!" to Aleshia. Aleshia was so caught off guard by the force of the command that she did stop. The lion, Ariel stopped in front of the girl, looked to Logan and Logan nodded to him. The lion bent down, picked up the trembling girl by the back of her dress like he would pick up a cub and handed her into the arms of her trembling father. The lion then calmly walked over to stand beside Logan, sat on his haunches, and let out an ear shattering roar. The thunderous applause Aleshia had always feared erupted, and yet she found herself naturally joining in. From then on, Logan participated in all the animal acts. It might be Aleshia who ordered Ariel to open wide his jaws, but it was Logan who confidently placed his head into the mouth of the lion.

PART 3

THE CONGREGATION

Chapter 9 - José and Jackknife

How do two walk together except that they have agreed? What we hold in common draws us together and becomes the bridge over our differences.

from "Wise Words and Proverbs"

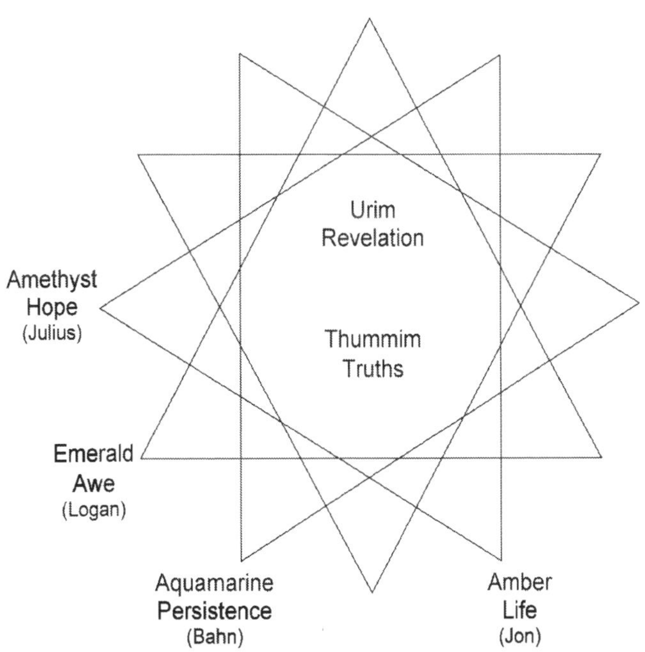

The drizzle seemed to penetrate right to the skin. It could not even be considered rain, soothing pitter patter, or pounding torrent washing everything clean, just the annoying mist that clung to everything, On nights like this the forsaken part of town called the Black Alley depressed even the stalwart soul. In its space a few tenants eked out a miserable existence, there were a couple of cheap taverns, and one pool hall called "the Raven's Den," the stomping ground for the youth of the area. About twenty years ago the Black Alley had been the battleground for rival gang wars. Later, it turned into a haven for the semi-rebellious subculture. Now all that remained was the residue of too many years of freedom or, maybe, just plain license, a thin shroud hiding despair and idle words. The drug they called "junk" was peddled freely. Some of the populace escaped into synthetic euphoria, but the rest of them trudged through their purposeless existence. Hope was not lost, though from all outward appearances, it seemed to have slipped away.

José considered himself an itinerant preacher. That is not to say that he had a parish of his own. The whole world was his parish. He was simply his own form of religious nonconformism. He worked as a common laborer for a construction company, a job that he had held now for a few years. His foreman seemed a little puzzled as to why José kept working at that job. Although he worked hard and had not missed a day of work because of sickness, why would a college educated man with a degree in biological science want to spend his life as a construction worker? Even more odd, after being in town only a few months, he started hanging around with the wrong sort of crowd. He was a preacher. Everybody knew that and if you asked him he would tell you. However, he did not seem to act hypocritically. He just hung around with what most people consider the undesirable characters of society. Almost every Friday and Saturday night you would find him down at the Raven's Den, shooting pool with the young dope heads. At first the kids pegged him as a narcotics agent because he did not swear, smoke, or use any of the dope. However, after a while they decided he was just square. As he continued to come down to the Raven's Den, they soon recognized him and even began saying, "Hi." After a few months they even gave him a nickname. They called him "The Saint." He seemed to rather enjoy it. They of course, found out that he was a preacher and assumed that was why he was a square. One of the nice things about The Saint, he was never too busy to listen to you. Soon he listened more than he played pool. He even gave away his pool cue. That probably broke the ice. Up until then he had seemed content to just be tolerated when he came down twice a week to play pool. He knew most of the regulars by name, but one younger kid especially interested him. His name was Todd, although he went by the nickname Jackknife.

Somehow José found out the date of Jackknife's birthday. He came down to the Raven that night with his pool cue all wrapped up as a present. Jackknife did not know what to do when José handed him this box, saying, "Happy birthday." His stunned look turned to outright shock when José said, "Well, open it!" Slowly he did, unveiling José's three-piece pool cue, case, weights, and all. Suddenly Jackknife ran outside and didn't return all night. Somebody said he had been crying. He acted like he had never received a present in his entire life. Well, actually, he had not. Jackknife carried the pool cue everywhere after that. That event seemed to precipitate the kids fully accepting The Saint, rather than just tolerate him. And some of the kids began to talk, really talk, to José. He would not say much, but what he did say more often than not, concerned his friend Jesus. Because of the pool cue, Jackknife found José the night his sister got hurt. Well, there was nowhere else to turn.

Jackknife's sister Judy was blonde and a little on the pretty side. Of course she wore too much makeup, and her skirts were too short, but only to draw attention away from her eyes. She thought her eyes were a little too small and narrow, keeping her face from being really pretty. She took dope like most of the rest of the kids. One thing for sure, she had not shared Jackknife's recent infatuation with The Saint. As far as she was concerned he was so square that it made her sick.

And so on this cold, depressing night, with a drizzling rain, Judy got hurt. No one meant for it to happen. Some of the kids had gone up to the tenements to have what they considered a little party. It took place in one of the older guy's apartment. A lot of them were smoking pot and some of them were dropping other stuff. Judy, of course, always at the scene of the action, had dropped something and had began having a bad trip. She began crying, and crying, and crying some more. One of the other partygoers got upset, being on a bad trip of his own. He turned towards Judy, telling her to shut up. She just kept crying and crying, and soon the other guy was on his feet shouting at her to shut up. The rest of the kids in the room, at least those still in some semblance of their right mind, watched in amazement as she cried and the other fellow yelled. Judy cried, and pleaded as though she wanted something. Whatever it was, all she got was a tremendous slap across the face that knocked her down into a low coffee table.

Jackknife saw her limp and still. He ran to her side. He did not retaliate, he did not even take his pool cue, just turned and ran out of the room and down the stairs, all the way to the Raven's Den. There he found The Saint sitting by himself in a booth in the back. Jackknife practically dragged him back to the tenement, explaining what happened along the way. José knelt beside the pretty little blonde, lying there like a rag doll tossed aside. She was breathing okay, her pulse strong, although rapid. What worried José was the small, bleeding wound in the backside of her head. Still kneeling he looked up at the ceiling of the rundown apartment and proceeded to talk as though someone was up there in the ceiling. "Jesus, help me!" Jackknife stood there dumbfounded. It was the first time he'd ever heard The Saint pray. Sure, José talked about God being alive and concerned with individuals, but when he prayed, he actually prayed as though he thought someone was there listening. José then walked up to the fellow who had slapped Judy, shook him out of his stupor, and asked him for his car keys.

Replying rather hazily and hesitantly he said "They are in my coat pocket." and pointed towards a jacket that was over a nearby chair. José did not own a car, although it would appear he could easily afford one.

He quickly shouted out the words, "Todd, get his keys!" at Jackknife while he bent over and easily lifted the young girl in his arms. While they were going to the car Jackknife noted something about The Saint that he had never seen before. The Saint walked with a slight but definite limp.

They drove to a hospital not far from the Black Alley and the tenements. Though by no means the most modern of the general hospitals, it did run a 24-hour emergency room. They walked through the emergency room door.

The hospital chaplain asked The Saint, "Father Franco, what's the matter?"

"One of the kids got hurt," was his only reply as he laid her on a hospital cart and relinquished her to an orderly. The two clergyman spoke to each other for just a moment then parted. José guided Jackknife by the arm into one of the two chairs at the admitting desk. He greeted the admitting clerk with smile and a simple, "Hi Lois." The Saint sure seem to know his way around this hospital.

José never talked much about himself. Down at the Raven's Den he always listened, rather than tooted his own horn. So no one down there really knew much about him except that he was a preacher, and that he showed up on Friday and Saturday nights.

"You been here before?" Jackknife finally got up the nerve to ask.

"Oh, yes, I am a volunteer chaplain here a couple nights a week."

Then he settled down to answering the clerk's questions. José assumed that Judy and Jackknife had no parents, and of course, no insurance. So he was not too surprised at Jackknife's quizzical look when the clerk asked who would pay the bill. Jackknife had already been impressed at what José had done to help them, covering for them as far as the dope party and the fight was concerned. He told them only that Judy had fallen, and he had gone to the trouble of getting her down there rather than calling the police or an ambulance.

But what really surprised him were the words, "Lois, put me down as the guarantor."

"What's that mean?" asked Jackknife.

"That means that I will see that the bill gets paid." he simply replied. Todd sat there with his mouth wide open, until he realized it. Then The Saint said, "Todd, why don't you take a seat in the waiting room while I try to see how they're doing with her."

José appeared to be on a first name basis with most of the Emergency Room personnel, for he headed straight towards the intern on duty. He returned several minutes later with the semblance of a story, saying the x-ray showed a fracture and possible concussion, but permanent effects were unknown at this point. "The really dangerous thing," the intern had explained "is the fact that she was on drugs." That made it impossible to tell what contribution they might have to the severity of her condition. In any event they were going to admit her for observation.

About half an hour later, they saw her in her room. Her head was bandaged and she was still unconscious, but all of her vital signs remained stable. The nurse said that she would probably sleep through the night, so José told Jackknife what he wanted him to do. "Todd, I want you to take the car back to the tenement. Then go to my house. Here's the keys and the address. Get some sleep. If there's any change in her condition I will let you know. In any event, I will call you in the morning. Oh, there's food in the refrigerator and cupboards if you're hungry. Feel free to eat what you like." Jackknife had been a typical rebellious teenager and even now was not used to taking orders from any adult, but he had a firmly grounded admiration for The Saint and being emotionally drained appreciated someone else making decisions for him. Jackknife bent over Judy and softly kissed her forehead. He then silently left the room and the hospital.

Jackknife did not really know what he expected The Saint's home to be like, but he would not have imagined what he found. It was a small house in what people still called the bad part of town. The adequate yard contained a fairly good-sized vegetable garden in the back and a large fir tree over in one corner. At the other end of the yard spread a beautiful maple tree. A white picket fence surrounded the light green house. Its trim was a darker, almost forest green. Flowers grew on each side of the front door, highlighted by red rose bushes. The porch light was on. As he put the keys into the lock and turned it, he heard a low growl from behind the door. "I didn't know The Saint had a dog," Jackknife thought to himself. As he slowly began to open the door the growl became more prominent, then the phone rang, and the growl stopped. Jackknife opened the door.

The dog looked like some kind of shepherd mix. His coal black fur ran from his toes on up to his only markings, a white cross that ran across his chest and down his belly. He stood by the ringing telephone, teeth barred in a low growl while he kept his eyes steadily on Jackknife. Jackknife advanced towards the ringing telephone slowly with his hand outstretched, palm extended. His already strained nerves threatened to snap, and the raw fear of the dog had him nearly paralyzed. If not for the constant reassurance of the ringing phone, he probably would have turned around. Finally he reached the phone. His one hand still extended palm downwards towards the dog, he slowly lifted the receiver to his ear with the other hand.

"Hello?" Jackknife said softly.

The voice on the line replied, "Oh, hello, Todd. I forgot to tell you about Adrian."

"Adrian?" Todd shuddered a little.

"Yes, my dog, who is no doubt standing about three feet away from you and growling."

Jackknife looked at the dog and then put the phone back to his ear.

"Todd? Put the phone down and stand back from it."

Jackknife obeyed, laying the phone gently down on its side, and stepping back a few steps.

Adrian took his eyes off Jackknife for the first time since he entered the house and looked at the phone. Then he began to wag his tail as he walked near the phone. Jackknife almost expected him put it to his ear, but instead he sniffed. He appeared to listen for a few moments and walked over to a rug that lay next to the red brick fireplace and laid down.

Jackknife cautiously walked back to the phone and picked it up to hear, "I told Adrian that you are okay. He will probably warm up to you now. Judy's still sleeping and everything seems to be fine. How about you? Are you okay?"

Jackknife replied slowly, but said, "Yes, I guess."

"Oh, one more thing Todd, Adrian is sort of my alarm clock in the reverse. He won't let me in bed until I have prayed with him, so when he jumps up on top of the bed and will not let you get in, just kneel beside the bed and pray. Pray for Judy. I think she could use it. Good night."

Jackknife reluctantly replied, "Good night," as he hung up the phone. Pray? He could not remember if he had ever prayed. He was not sure he knew how to pray, and he had only just heard The Saint pray tonight. At first it had startled him, because The Saint seemed to be talking to somebody he expected to answer. Well, anyway, before he went to bed he could use a sandwich or something.

With that, he began to explore the exceptionally well kept house. It appeared to have been dusted and vacuumed recently. He sat on the gold tweed sofa and surveyed the living room. The sofa was only fairly comfortable, probably because it looked like it could be changed into a bed. The living room had been painted a light tan almost golden in color, the windows trimmed in a darker gold. The fireplace, next to which Adrian lay, took center stage. Above it hung a large picture portraying the crucifixion. The face of Jesus on the cross captivated Jackknife's attention and for some reason, deep down inside of him, there stirred up an emotion that cried out, "You are killing the wrong man!" A love seemed to pour out of the expression on Jesus' face and drove Jackknife's eyes down to the bold caption that read, "I die that you might live." The words did not seem to make any real sense to Jackknife, but he promised himself he would ask the Saint later what it all meant.

He moved across the room to the kitchen, larger than it looked at first glance. The white tile floor, with light walnut stained cabinets and simple, white appliances, matched the living room well, which helped the decor since they faced each other. Jackknife located some bread, butter, mayonnaise, luncheon meat, and a couple of half gallons of milk. He fixed himself a sandwich. When he turned around, he found Adrian had silently crept up behind him. "Are you hungry, big fella?" He dropped him a small piece of meat. Adrian picked up the meat and carried it over by a small dinette table where two bowls sat on a plastic mat. He dropped it into the bowl, then devoured the meat, some water, and turned around to face Jackknife who, with sandwich and a glass of milk in hand, went to explore the rest of the small house.

He found a small and spartan bathroom next to the kitchen. A similarly equipped, but larger bedroom shared a wall with the living room and also had a fireplace, apparently the backside of the one in the living room. Papers cluttered a study desk next to the fireplace. The desk was the only place in the entire house that was not completely neat and tidy, and even it could not be considered messy by most standards. A number of books, a couple of which appeared to be written in foreign languages, lay open to different pages on the desk. He recognized a Bible. Floor-to-ceiling books filled about half of one wall, almost all of which appeared to be about the Bible. A double bed and two dressers stood against the opposite wall with a closet between them. Jackknife felt the room quite homey with its light blue walls, accented by deep blue carpet and a blue-and-white bedspread. He opened a door to the final room to reveal a smaller bedroom done in shades of green containing one twin bed, desk, small chest of drawers, and closet. This was obviously the guest room. Having finished his perusal of the house and also his milk and sandwich, Jackknife realized how tired he felt.

"Where should he sleep?" Apparently The Saint did not care. As he turned to leave the guest room Jackknife almost tripped over Adrian who had silently come to his side again. He reached down to pet the dog and Adrian did not shy away, but began to slowly wag his tail. He patted him hesitantly and then, when he saw he how much the dog enjoyed it, vigorously. "You like that big fella? You like that?" His more rapid tail wagging removed all doubt about the apparent answer. "Well, Adrian, if I go to sleep here in the guest room, will you make me pray first?" He stripped to his shorts, flung his clothing across the chair that sat by the desk, and began to turn back the covers. Suddenly, he found the large black dog astride his bed. "Come on, Adrian, have a heart, I don't know how to pray." The dog only looked at him as though he were ready to play.

Reluctantly, Todd knelt beside the bed, rested his elbows on the bed, and folded his hands. At this point Adrian laid down on the bed with his head cradled in his front paws and promptly closed his eyes as if he was actually going to pray. Jackknife was wondering if Adrian actually expected him to pray out loud, when he suddenly felt overwhelmed by a strange unfamiliar sensation. It felt like someone else had entered the room. He looked slowly around him. He saw, of course, no one. Yet he still felt this... presence. He knew someone was there. He closed his eyes and the feeling seemed to intensify.

"Um, God?" He could almost feel this presence listening. "I have heard The Saint talk about you down at the Raven saying that you love me. Do you love me? You don't know me very well, if you do. The Saint says you love me anyway. Do you? Nobody loves Jackknife, except maybe Judy. But The Saint says you love me, so I guess maybe you do. God, I feel rotten, can you help me? Can I ever be free? Please help me."

For the first time in his life Todd felt a spark of hope. "God, please help my sister. Please let her be all right." He was pleading now even beginning to cry. He had not cried like this in a long time except when The Saint had given him his pool cue. He let his innermost feelings come to the surface and wash over him. His feeling of lostness, his love for his sister, his need to know if God was really there. He began to cry uncontrollably. When finally subsided, he found Adrian licking his cheek. The presence left. He quietly climbed into bed. Then he had to get out again to turn off the light. He got under the covers, pulled some of them around his neck, and attempted to absorb the reassuring warmth. Soon he slept.

José spent the first few minutes after Todd left just sitting beside Judy's bed and waiting. What he waited for he did not know as she was still unconscious. He pulled his battered New Testament out of his back pocket and began to read. He read from the gospel of Mark and then switched to the book of Acts. Then went back to one of the Gospels again. Suddenly, the words leapt off the pages. There seemed to be a blazing fire going on in his heart and mind. He read how Jesus rebuked the fever in Peter's mother-in-law. He stopped reading and looked at Judy lying there unconscious. He looked back to the words. Could this be God trying to tell him something? He had witnessed the miraculous healing of drug addicts before and had even been used in the healing of a few, but nothing of this sort had happened since he had moved here. Now that he had begun to break the ice in some of the relationships with the addicts at the Raven, maybe the time was ripe for God to begin to do more. Yet in all of the healings that he had participated in, the addict had always been conscious and wanting help. What about Judy? Would God heal her as he did Peter's mother-in-law? He looked at the words in the worn New Testament again.

"And Jesus rebuked the fever." Slowly and trembling, at least inwardly if not outwardly, José dropped to his knees at the bedside. As he knelt there he could almost hear someone whispering in his ear.

A familiar voice said, "You fool, get off your knees! What if someone sees you?" He bowed his head, folded his hands on the chair, and began to pray silently. From somewhere down the hall came the soft pad of someone walking towards the room. Again the voice seemed to speak to him, "See, someone's coming. Get up off your knees!"

He continued to pray. The nurse stepped into the room and stopped. After a moment he got up and turned around to face the nurse, somewhat startled to find her head still bowed in an attitude of prayer also. She opened her eyes and looked kindly into his. He did not recognize her. She was young for a nurse, perhaps a recent graduate.

She softly spoke, "Maybe you should get some sleep, Father." Apparently she knew him. He seemed hesitant to leave.

"Miss, you're a Christian?" he asked. The beginning of a smile touched her face as she nodded, "Do you believe God can heal people today?" he asked as he shifted his eyes from the nurse to the young girl in bed.

"Yes," she said. "He healed me about 10 years ago of a rather rare disease."

Somewhat startled, again, he now began to follow what had become an almost irresistible force carrying him along. He beckoned the nurse to come to the opposite side of the bed. Each of them took one of Judy's hands, and José lifted his eyes to the ceiling and spoke, "Father, I thank You for hearing me." Then he sternly looked at the girl, though not really at the girl, and spoke again barely above a whisper, "Demon, in the name of Jesus, I command you to release Judy! I command you to set her free and leave her alone. Come out of her in Jesus' name!"

A slight shudder shook Judy from head to foot, but other than that nothing visibly changed. Again, with a lift of his eyes upward and smiling he spoke, "Father, now guard and protect her by

Your Holy Spirit, and thank You." His eyes glistened with a tear, but he held it back.

He looked again at the nurse, "Excuse me miss, but I don't know your name."

She replied a little bashfully, "That's okay, I'm new here. My name is Christine Andrews."

One of the lab girls came to draw some blood samples for more testing and disturbed their quiet conversation. They walked out of the room together.

He extended his hand in a friendly gesture, "You can dispense with the Father, I'm just José." She gently shook his hand and they slowly walked to the nurse's station. "Could you please leave word that I'll be down in the chaplain's office and would like to be notified when Judy awakens?" She nodded her assent as he thanked her and walked briskly towards the stairs.

Trying to express only casual interest, Christine turned to the nurses in charge of the ward with the question, "Does that priest come here often?"

Seemingly uninterested, the older RN replied, "Oh, him? Yes, he's up here fairly often. A number of patients seem to really like him."

At least the hospital chaplain's office had a fairly comfortable couch. José knew this because he had often used it. He dialed the emergency room number,.

"Emergency room, Johnson RN," came the answer.

"May I please speak with Reverend Click if he's there?"

"Yes, just a moment," came the reply.

A fairly long pause and then, "Jim Click here," came the unusually bright voice.

"Jim, José here. I'm going to catch some shut eye in your office if it's okay."

"Sure, be my guest. How's the young girl?"

"Well, she's still unconscious, and I would appreciate your prayers."

"You know you got them, José," was the somewhat more serious reply.

"If they haven't called me by eight, could you wake me, Jim?"

"Sure José. I'll see you then, and if things settle down here I'll go up and look in on the little lady myself. What did you say her name was?"

"It's Judy Gillespie, and thanks a lot, Jim."

"No sweat," he replied and broke the connection.

As he slipped off his shoes and lay down on the couch the thought flashed through his mind, my dog Adrian is not here to remind me of my prayers. He prayed a short prayer thanking God for the day and for the inroads they made into the Raven's Den folk. Then he prayed for Judy and Todd. Pulling a blanket over himself that he had picked up on one of the other floors, he dropped off into a light sleep.

He found himself up and halfway to the telephone before the first ring completed, and picked it up in the middle of the second. "Hello?"

"José? This is Jim. I'm up here looking out for your interests and have been talking to the nurses. They say she is starting to come to, and they tell me she will be in the middle of drug withdrawal, so you better get up here."

José went into the bathroom connected to the chaplain's office, relieved himself, and splashed some cold water on his face. His evening's growth of beard would have to wait until later. He took the stairs two at a time reaching the fourth floor a little out of breath.

He met Jim at the nurses station. "I just left her. She's not awake yet, but she's been sleeping restlessly the last half an hour. They tell me she's in for an overdose." José nodded. "You sure work with a rough bunch, José. Well, I'll turn her over to you. I just put a cup coffee in there for you."

José smiled and extended his hand, "Thanks, Jim." They briefly shook hands and parted.

Judy appeared to be still resting comfortably when José entered the room. He noted a few changes, the nasal gastric tube had been removed and they had started an IV in her forearm. The removal of the nasal gastric tube boded well. It meant they felt that they had gotten rid of as much of the drugs from her stomach as possible. Her system had assimilated some, but the fact that they had started an IV in her arm said they were pretty sure they could balance the drug's effects. He looked at the bottle of IV solution at the head of the bed. "That's funny," he thought, "this is just a plain IV with no additives." Still a little puzzled he looked down at Judy again. She turned her head first to the left and then to the right. Cautiously he picked up her hand and cradled it in his. Her eyes blinked twice and she looked around.

"Judy?" She looked towards him. "Don't be frightened you are in a hospital."

She had raised herself partially on one elbow. "Who's there? Who are you?" she questioned looking at José.

"It's me, José, The Saint," using the nickname the kids called him. "You've had a bad trip and hurt yourself, but you'll be all right."

She still looked around the room as if trying to focus her vision. She took her hand from José and then put it in front of her face. "What time is it?" José glanced at his watch. "It sure is dark in here" she said drowsily. "I can't even see my hand." Before José could reply she dropped off into a restful sleep. A cold chill ran up José's back and neck. At almost seven in the morning the bright morning sunlight filled Judy's room, and she had acted as though shrouded in darkness. He sucked in a short breath. Could she be… blind?

José quickly stepped out of the room and rapidly walked to the nurses station. Christine's extremely cheerful smile met him.

"José," she beamed and spoke softly clutching his arm, "We have gotten back the lab reports and there's not a trace of drugs in her bloodstream. If she was going to go through withdrawal, she'd be in the midst of it now. I think she's been healed."

It took that long for Jose's frightened look to register through her joy.

"What's the matter, is something wrong?"

He stammered out, "I think so" and turned her towards the room. Though his evidence was inconclusive, he told her what he feared as they walked quickly back to it. Judy must have heard them enter, because she sat up as they did.

"Good morning Judy." Christine's greeting was cheerful, though superficially so. "I'm your nurse."

Judy looked in her direction and squinted trying to see them. "Would you please turn on the light, so that I can see you?" she asked innocently.

"The lights are on, Judy," José replied as a tear glistened on his cheek.

Two days passed before she recovered from the shock of discovering her blindness and finding out she would live the rest of her life in darkness. After that, the story that José told her of how he had prayed, and she'd been delivered of having to go through withdrawal interested her most. In fact, she responded by swearing off drugs. And yet, the puzzling fact of her blindness remained. After the nurse had checked her eyes with a flashlight and found they neither responded nor did she see the light. She quickly called the doctor. They repeated a number of x-rays, did miscellaneous other tests and scans, but all they could say was that she was blind. It appeared to have been caused by a combination of drugs and the blow to the back of her head. Either of the two could have caused the blindness, if severe enough. It seemed likely that the two in conjunction had been enough to do so. From what they could tell, there existed no cure. Except for her blindness, Judy seemed to be perfectly well and even in good spirits. José attributed this to the fact that the second evening after they had discovered her blindness, something else wonderful had happened. In the quietness of her hospital room, Judy had met Jesus herself.

Todd had responded well to all of this. Her healing disturbed him some. Why would God deliver her from the drug withdrawal yet leave her blind? José did not have any clear answer, other than, "He is not obligated to work in the ways we think He should. He is God, after all, and we are not." Judy and Todd had lots of questions, so the three of them began to meet together.

José and Todd would read Scripture, they would all talk a lot, and they would pray. Soon, Todd shared with them that he, too, had met Jesus and was now trying to follow Him as best as he could. After Judy was released from the hospital they continued to meet once or twice a week, usually at Judy and Todd's place. Their friendship grew and their fellowship deepened.

A few months later José asked them if they would like to go meet a friend of his, Jon, who had a farm outside of town. It would provide the opportunity for them to meet with some other like-minded people that might help them grow in this new journey in an atmosphere of community. José spoke of it so highly and so often that one night after prayer Judy and Todd said, "Sure, let's go visit your friend's farm and meet with the folks there." Pleased with their decision, José made plans for a visit.

Chapter 10 - Our Gatherings

A flock of geese flies in formation to fly further together. They take turns leading. They honk encouragement to one another.

from "Abigail's book of Avian Lore"

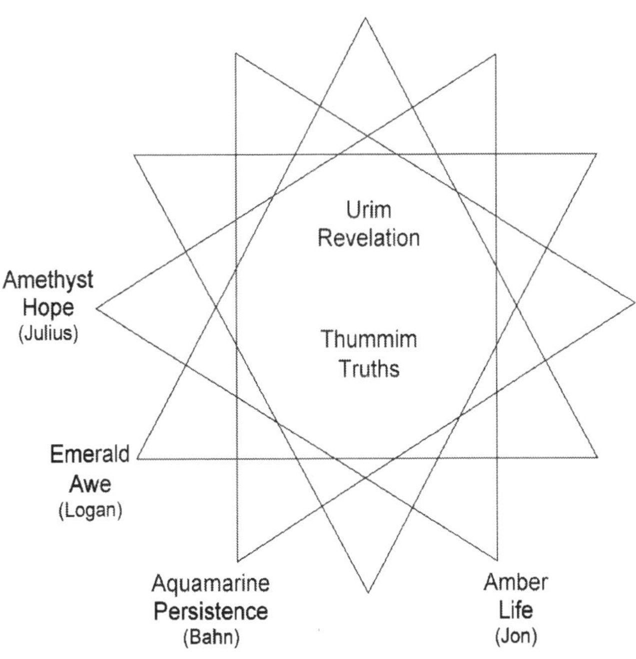

The congregation consisted of a rather ragtag band of misfits, mostly from the circus. Jon pastored them, although not ordained by any of the state's organizations or representatives. Their group of supposed dissidents existed outside the confines of organized religion. They simply considered themselves followers of the Liberator. Jon had met Julius the clown after one of the circus performances. He had simply wanted to tell him how much he appreciated his part and contribution to a wonderful experience for all of those in attendance, but it had led to a lunch date, a friendship, and the founding of a fledgling congregation there. Julius told Jon, in the course of their conversations, that the circus performers had no one for spiritual support and guidance. So, Jon became that for them. He became their pastor. Julius the clown and his adopted daughter Anna, Logan the dwarf, and the trapeze artists Bruno and his wife, Natalia all attended. When they finally moved their meetings to the farm they also included Mary, Jon's wife, and the farm workers: Juan Carlos, Maria, and all of their children. Those at the farm lived in a self-sustaining manner out beyond the suburbs. They raised their own food, had their own well, produced their own electricity and could, basically, survive without intervention from the city or the government. This fact neither the city nor the government appreciated.

Because the state church had not authorized them, they had to be careful how they operated. Without licensing and sanctioning the state automatically suspected and saw the congregation as a threat. What they stood for mattered less than their complete independence from the state. Those who worked outside the compound provided enough income to pay the local taxes. The rest of them flew below the radar, so to speak. Their simple services included worship, scripture, teaching and prayer. While they considered Jon their pastor, they could all lead and teach, and did so from time to time. Their life together provided the fodder for sharing grace, truth, and righteousness. They did not formally or overtly proselytize. That was forbidden to all but those licensed by the state. They merely shared their faith when they could, lived it out in the marketplace, and slowly grew in numbers. José (called The Saint downtown) had brought with him Judy and her brother Todd. Judy and Anna quickly became friends, partly because they were both blind, but more because they simply enjoyed one another's company. Bahn showed up one day, though Jon had not seen him for what seemed like ages.

"Bahn, it seems like forever. How long has it been?" Jon asked.

"Too many moons and even more suns." Bahn always talked like that.

"Where have you been, and what have you been doing?" Jon continued.

"Oh, walking to and fro on the earth, seeing what it has become," he countered.

"And...," Jon said. Although Bahn talked almost in riddles, Jon had known him a long enough to interpret most of them.

"Evil waxes strong most everywhere. There is little of light, truth, or life out there. Most, especially the young, are being led astray and into bondage. Few worship and there is little awe of God. Mostly, they give themselves to pleasure, technology, and the pursuit of vanity." expressed Bahn with a frown.

Jon thought he was building up a head of steam for a complete diatribe, but he stopped there and asked for some tea. Like most things, they made their own. In fact much of what they had learned in order to become independent from the world system they had learned from Bahn, who was one of Jon's most trusted friends and mentors.

As a growing congregation, they found that having regular, weekly meetings in homes helped them stay under the radar and still share life together. They only met all together on the last day of each month. Since that day shifted in the week each month, it made it more difficult for some to attend, but it also made it difficult for the authorities to track. Everyone showed up at different times during the day, but most of them arrived in time for a late evening meal and a time of sharing and praying. Only standing room remained in their expanded living and dining room, even with all the furniture moved out. They had tried meeting in the barn, but the logistics of getting and keeping it clean enough, especially for the kids, were daunting. They did not want to build another building and draw too much attention from the authorities. They assumed the regular drone traffic flying over their place belonged to the government's ongoing surveillance of them. So, they had decided that they would expand the basement slowly and by hand. It would take quite a while, but it presented the best option, all things considered. It would also draw the congregation closer together as a community. Everyone would participate in the project in some manner.

Chapter 11 - Jon's Wife, Mary

What is life, but a passing cloud blown away
by the wind to reveal the sun.
What is death, but the endless darkness of a lonely night
except when the smile and warm embrace of the King dispels it.
from the "Musings of the Seer"

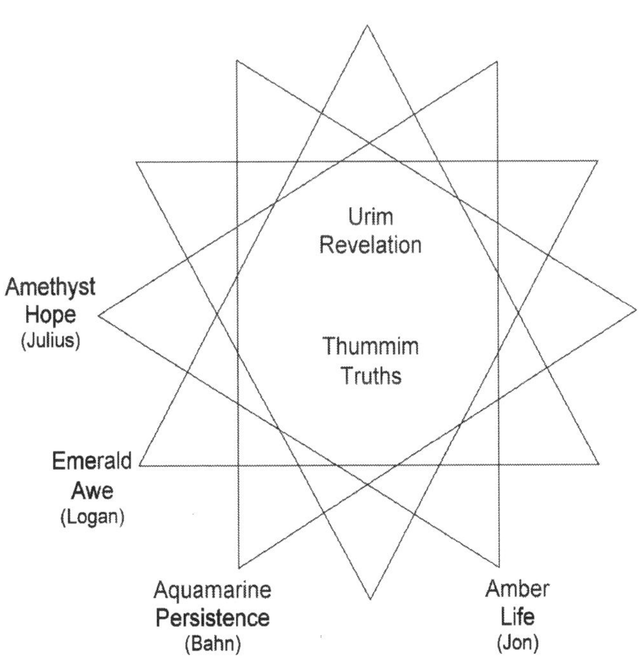

Jon met Mary in Bible School. He had always dreamed of helping people and believed that he would be able to help them best as a pastor. He knew that he would need a good sound Biblical education and had enrolled in a Bible school for that purpose. Over the course of two years they studied the entire Bible, less the duplicate books: Kings, but not Chronicles, not all of the Gospels. There he met a group of people that obviously had a quality of life different than his own. They had a personal relationship with Jesus Christ. He only knew about Him. Before too long he took advantage of the opportunity to meet Him. Jesus transformed Jon's life, radically altering Jon's personality. Because "He who knew him best, loved him most," Jon could now love and accept himself. He no longer needed to be afraid of what people thought of him. It probably made Jon a little reckless, hopefully in a good way. Jon and some of his friends took their instruments (guitars, horns, etc.) and serenaded the girls' dormitory. Jon joined choir. He even began to take on some leadership positions which he would have never done before. He met Mary. Her boyfriend had proposed to her, but she had put him off for a year while she dated others to make sure that he was truly the one. Then she met Jon. He impulsively and recklessly proposed on the second date. She responded firmly but nicely, "Are you crazy?" He took that as a "No!" It took another year for her to finally say no to the other guy and yes to Jon. They married right out of school when Jon received an initial pastorate. Unfortunately, they could not have children, but that did open up a significant number of other possibilities. They did some mission work around the world, helping people in a variety of settings and situations. They built houses, Jon taught classes, they did medical work: all of this greatly expanding their horizons. They became more than religious denominationalists. They became true followers of the Liberator, Jesus, and ended up separating from what became the State church.

While Jon was the visionary, Mary was the practical and detailed person that helped make those dreams come true. She love order, but not simply for order's own sake. She loved order for the harmony that it created. She had the gift that the Chinese would call Feng Shui, the ability to create environments of peace, safety, and security. She also brought peace and harmony into relationships, perfect for the role of a pastor's wife. All of their giftings they brought to the founding of the congregation at the farm, itself a miraculous occurrence. They had often talked and prayed about doing something outside of the city independent of the world system, and a friend of a friend knew of a few acres of property that included some animals, buildings, an orchard, a large garden, and some farmable land. The current owner wanted it put to good use, offered it at a good price, and the finances were miraculously available. Lo and behold they instantly became farmers and ranchers. The two bunkhouses became men's and women's dorms and the main house had enough room for at least two families since Jon and Mary had no children. Their job, with Bahn's help, became learning to live off of the land, and their ministry turned into teaching others how to do the same. Jon's long association with the circus gave those folks a place of retreat during the off season, and they all became one big happy family.

A number of wonderful years and in the midst of a thriving personal economy, tragedy struck. In the middle of the night Jon awoke to Mary crying out in pain. She seemed to be having a terrible headache. She had been having them off and on for a while, but this night seemed different. Initially, Jon figured it for a spiritual rather than physical attack. However, when he called Bahn from the bunkhouse and into their bedroom, Bahn took one look around and whispered with authority, "It's not spiritual! Call an aid car." The Emergency Medical Technicians arrived within minutes and Jon was pleasantly surprised that the first EMT into their bedroom was an acquaintance. Fred had visited the farm on a number of occasions, presumably to purchase unadvertised produce; more often than not, he wanted to just chat. The EMT's took Mary off to the city hospital where the doctors pronounced her "dead on arrival" due to a brain aneurysm. Both Jon and Mary had willed their bodies to science. So, after a short goodbye to the empty shell that used to house Mary's soul and spirit, the university whisked her off to be used in whatever way they saw fit. Two weeks later Jon received a small urn of her cremated remains and a letter from the university thanking him for the scientific use of her body.

They held a small gathering of those who knew and loved Mary. Jon probably should have been more disconsolate, but, even as he shared that evening, he did not believe in her death. This was not denial, but a firm belief that she had only moved out of her current body and would one day take up residence in another, much better one. After the service they spread her ashes across the large garden. While not particularly legal, he knew it was what she wanted. Life began again, a little emptier at the center of things, but what else could they all do? Mary had been so much a part of all of their dreams and plans. Now they tried to fulfill them with somewhat diminished enthusiasm. Eventually, even the enthusiasm returned as their dreams, and the Liberator, helped them navigate past their grief.

PART 4

CONNECTIONS

Chapter 12 - The Woodworker and Piper

A man found a treasure hidden in a field. When he found it, he covered it back up. Then, in his joy, he went and sold all that he had and purchased the field and its treasure. Matthew 13:44

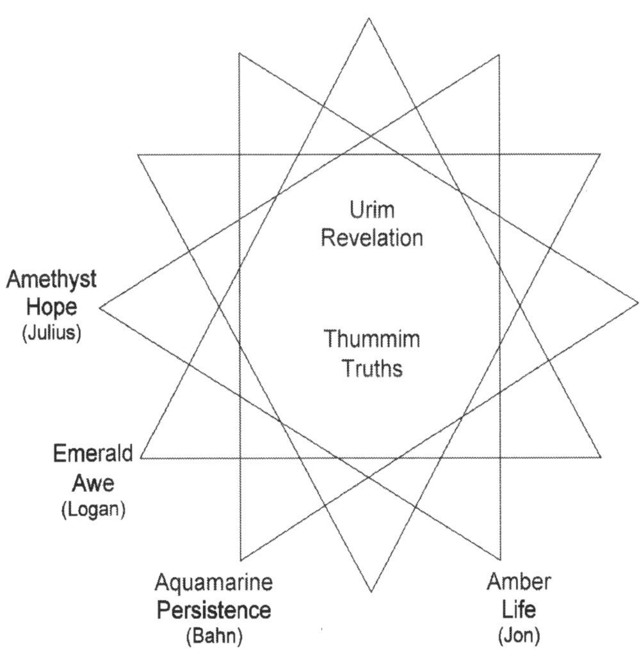

A woodworker by trade, he spied her one day as he passed the town's garbage dump. It reminded him of the story about someone finding a treasure hidden in a field. At least he did not have to buy the garbage dump in order to take her with him. He could just take her home, clean her up, and attempt to restore her. To the world she might be something discarded into the trash, but to him she was something quite different, something of promise. Each night after he came home from work he would take her off the shelf and spend some time lovingly working on her restoration. Painstakingly, slowly, he removed the accumulated dirt, grime, and filth that she had collected over the years. Each night when he finished he would place her back on the shelf. It seemed she spent most of her life waiting on the shelf. The time in his hands each day felt wonderful although sometimes unpleasant with the scraping, prodding, poking, but at the end of each day she felt lighter, and freer as he lovingly placed her back on the shelf. Then one evening he pronounced, "Ah…, she is finished!" and placed her back on the shelf. That next morning he left the window open. When he returned from work a sparrow had made its nest next to her. Surprised but pleased, he left the nest untouched. Each morning with the sun's rise, the sparrow sang her melody clearly and purely from the nest. He often wondered if he could capture the melody. Eventually he could hum it a little, and one evening he picked her up and began to play her. Before he lay his head on his pillow that evening, together they had captured the sparrow's song.

People still tell how on the night of the great feast, the wedding feast of the king, the old carpenter stood up and unexpectedly put a little pipe to his lips and played the melody that became the people's national anthem. Named "The Song of Deliverance," "The Return of All Things Good," and many other names, to him it will always be "The Sparrow's Song."

Many years have passed, and the carpenter as well. Kingdoms fell, rose, and fell again, and the world entered the times of darkness. There seemed to be little hope in the world. One day a young woman, still pure in an age of moral corruption searched through another garbage dump looking for a few scraps of food when she came upon a small wooden pipe flute. Amusing, that her name was Piper, and she had now found a pipe. She took it home, if you could call the boxes she lived in a home, and lovingly cleaned it up the best she could. Then she put it to her lips and attempted to play the little pipe. Once again, after so many years, the earth heard the sparrow's song and the ground began to shake. It split beneath her feet to reveal a sparkling yellow topaz, vibrating joyfully to the tune of the pipe. Still playing the pipe with one hand, she lifted the stone with the other, consumed by a joy that exceeded any she had ever known. Over the years she had learned to be content with her simple life, but now joy overwhelmed her-just her, the flute, the stone, and a song for the King.

Chapter 13 - Aaron and José

The Urim and the Thummim were unique from the twelve. More than simple stones of fire and power, they held a special place in the breastplate of the luminescent one.

Just as revelation and truth form the foundation of wisdom, the Urim and the Thummim made him unlike any in all of creation.

from the "Sacred Book of the Stars"

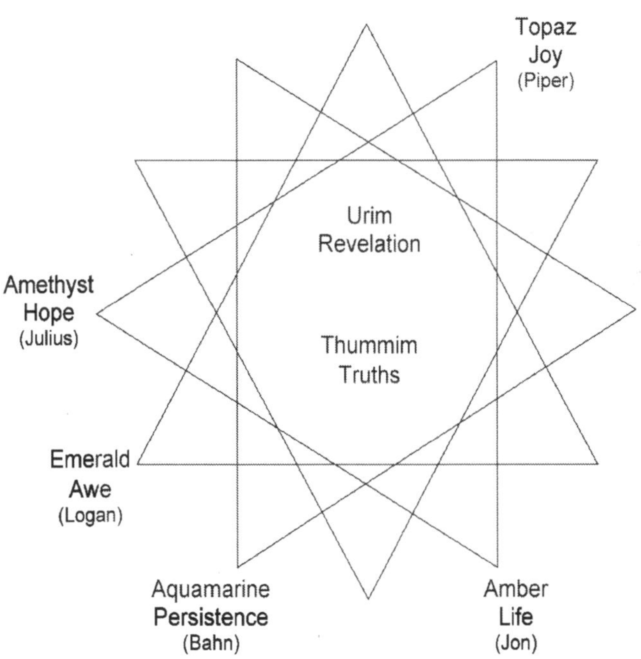

If you asked Aaron Elias, "Do you hear voices?" he would reply, "Yes." If you asked him if he thought that odd, he would answer, "No, we all hear voices in our head." And then he would add, "If someone says, 'I don't hear voices in my head. I tell them, "That's one of the voices." His single goal in life was to only say and do what God told him or showed him. If you asked him about his progress towards this goal, he would smile and say, "Much further than when I started." When asked, "Why did you show up at the Raven's Den?" he replied, "God told me to come here last week. It took me some time to put my affairs, small as they are, in order and travel here." He carried a large rucksack which contained the sum total of his affairs. He met José on his first Friday night. Aaron was standing near the pool table, so undistinguished and silent that everyone easily ignored him. At least until he spoke. His voice carried an unmistakable authority.

José, The Saint, had called out his shot, "14 in the corner pocket," as he stroked the cue ball.

Aaron added, "And 16 in the side pocket."

Everyone looked at him and then quickly back to the table. Sure enough the cue ball hit the 14 ball into the corner pocket, bounced off the cushion to lightly tap the 16 ball which slowly moved toward and fell into the side pocket. An audible silence fell on those watching the game. Many of them just shook their heads. "A lucky guess," they thought to themselves.

Ed lined up his ball and called out, "7 in the far corner."

After he stroked it, Aaron said nonchalantly, "Nope."

It missed the pocket slightly. "Another lucky guess," many thought. This continued for some time, until Ed had lost the game. Ed pointed to Aaron, "That guy put a hex on me!" He swore angrily and left the Den.

The Saint came over to Aaron, extending his right hand as he said, "José." Aaron looked at his extended hand. It was almost as if he wanted to see how long José would hold it out there unanswered.

"I know who you are," Aaron whispered with a smile and then shook José's hand. "Aaron," he said still smiling. His smile was quite disarming.

They found a table, sat down, and ordered drinks. José ordered a diet soda, Aaron an earthy iced tea.

José chuckled, "I didn't know they even made an earthy iced tea. In fact, what is an earthy iced tea?"

Aaron smiled again, "I don't know, but it sounds good and I'm an earthy kind of guy."

"So, how did you do that, call all those shots and missed shots?" José tried not to show too much interest.

"You might call it a gift, but I would call it just paying attention," Aaron said frankly. "I wasn't particularly trying to attract attention to myself, but I was trying to attract your attention." He continued, "You see, José, I have been led to you."

"Is it some kind of prophetic gifting?' José asked.

"Some might call it that, but again, I would simply call it a good listening skill," said Aaron. They talked well into the wee hours of the morning.

In the end José asked Aaron to move in with him, "I have a guest room, but you probably already know that being a prophet," José chuckled again. Aaron did not want to impose, but José convinced him he would not be.

True to Aaron's desire or wish, he was no inconvenience, and José's dog Adrian loved him. Aaron proved quite a help. He quickly learned José's habits, likes, and dislikes and anticipated them. He kept the guest room spotless and all of his stuff stowed away neatly yet ready to pack up and leave at a moment's notice. He spent his days walking the streets, perusing the shops, attentive to people and their needs. He often prayed for people on the street, in the stores, everywhere he could and, though never obtrusive or showy, with amazing results. Because of his simple goal to follow God's leading, his prayers were wonderfully and often answered. Besides being prophetic, able to tell people things that he could in no way know naturally, he would often heal them. He did not pray for their healing, he just healed them. He quickly pointed out that God healed them, but often from his simple word, command, or just touching them, they would be healed. Then he would smile and walk away. Aaron never made it about himself, he was just an instrument, a humble, unobtrusive, and obedient vehicle through which God worked. However, he did begin to draw attention. People began showing up at the store just because they had heard that a man there would pray for you. Then, after he did, they felt so much better, they would stay and do some shopping. Although it got to be a bit disruptive; not the line at the cash register, or the line at the customer service counter, but the line of people waiting for Aaron to pray for them. An overzealous security guard called the police. Two uniformed officers showed up at the store and were shown the problem by the guard. The two officers snuck up behind Aaron and just observed for a few minutes. Those waiting in line were focused so entirely on what happened as Aaron spoke that they did not even notice the officers. The officers finally had enough.

One of them spoke authoritatively, "What is going on here?"

Aaron stopped praying, turned around, and replied, "What can I do for you, officers?"

The one smiled and mockingly said, "I have this pain," pointing to his shoulder.

Aaron did not smile. He just stepped forward, placed his hand on the man's shoulder and, before the officer even had time to flinch, his eyes snapped shut and he crumpled to the floor. The other stepped back, reaching for his side arm.

"That won't be necessary," Aaron whispered with even more authority than the first officer had spoken. Aaron knelt down and lightly touched the officer on the forehead. His eyes fluttered open as Aaron spoke, "It's not a good idea to make fun of God. Come on, let me help you to your feet." As he helped him up, the first officer looked visibly shaken and the second officer frightened.

Aaron said again, "How may I help you, officers?"

The taller office, who had not been on the floor, took a deep breath and quietly said, "You need to stop what you are doing and leave the store."

Aaron countered with, "Because…"

The taller officer continued, "You are creating a public disturbance in violation of City Ordinance 5482 Section 9."

Aaron responded with, "I'm sorry." He turned and walked away while the two stunned officers stood there dumb-founded. Aaron shared the events of the day with José over supper and they both had a good laugh. Then they both realized they should take some preventative action before the authorities figured out where Aaron lived.

José said, "I have a friend who owns a farm out in the country. He does a good job of staying under the authorities' radar. I'm thinking we should go stay there for awhile. What do you think?"

Aaron asked, "Can we sleep on it and pray about it?"

They knelt there in the living room, elbows on the couch and prayed, then went to bed. When José awoke the next morning, Aaron already sat in the kitchen with Adrian at his feet, two cups of steaming tea placed on the table before him. José looked at the consternation on Aaron's face.

He asked. "What's up my friend?"

Aaron began slowly, "I'm not sure we have any idea what we are getting ourselves into, but I believe that you are right. We are to go to your friend's farm," he continued. "Last night I had a nearly apocalyptic dream. We may be moving into the end of days much sooner than any of us had anticipated. This farm is a joining place, a coming together of a small band of folks who are going to be instrumental in fighting the coming darkness. I also saw a refuge, a sanctuary, deep in the forest, a place of indescribable beauty and unbelievable power. God says this place is the launching point of many destinies!" Aaron's words, so powerful and spiritually pregnant, caused José to weep.

He replied, "Well let's pack our things and go!"

Aaron smiled, "I am already packed. I will make breakfast while you pack. Travel light, you won't need much." After eating, washing the dishes, and packing a lunch, the three of them set out for the farm.

PART 5

SIGNS OF THE TIMES

Chapter 14 - The Triparteum

...And there shall arise from among the princes of the world one who brings peace where there has never been peace before, the uniter of bloods and bloodlines...and he who was mortally wounded will reign over all the people...and he will restore the sacred sciences and worship the elemental forces...and none will dare to stand against him, until...

from the "Book of the Prophecies"

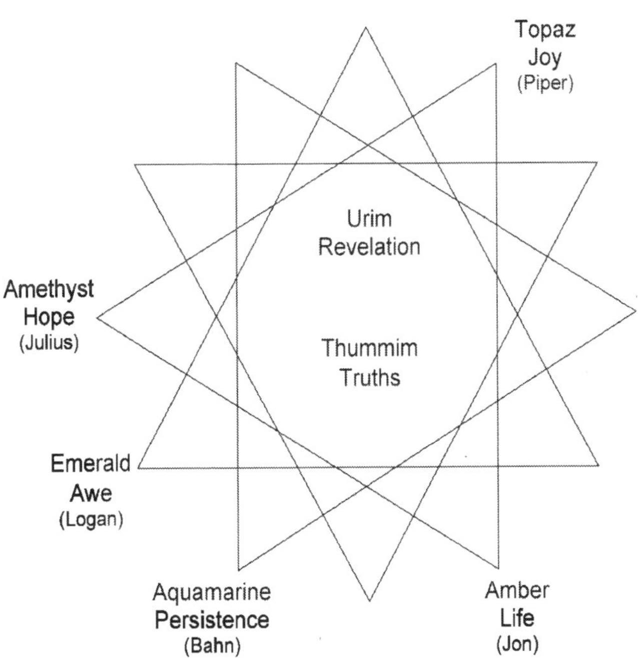

The furnace of cultural adversity birthed the Triparteum. Economic chaos and near extinction from global war threatened the entire planet until the leaders of government, finance, and religion came together and forged this unique international union. The council of the assembly consisted of single representatives from education, science, technology, politics, religion, the arts, military, and history, led by the Chancellor Adonis Ashereem. Born to an Arab father and a Jewish mother, Adonis most recently come to prominence as the architect of the Israeli/Palestinian peace accord, Selah. Only this accord had received unilateral support from all the other nations and had actually lasted the past three years without violation. It appeared to be the grounds for lasting peace in the Middle East and that was only his latest miracle. The religious sector actually wanted to canonize him for an earlier miracle. During the talks that ended up being the Selah accord, Adonis had been shot in the head by a Palestinian assassin. Rushed to the hospital, the doctors pronounced him dead on arrival. The assassin had been captured, had tried to commit suicide, but had been prevented from doing so. They imprisoned him in an Israeli fortress that a mob attacked later that evening, calling for his public execution. The Israeli military probably would have surrendered him to the mob the next day, if Adonis had not walked out of the hospital completely healed, gone to the fortress and on camera forgiven his attacker. Those three miracles: his recovery, his forgiveness of his attacker, and the signing of the peace accord, launched him into the chancellorship of the newly formed Triparteum council.

The establishment of the Triparteum had created an almost instantaneous international unity, universal peace, and economic recovery. Suddenly all divisions just melted away, crime seemed to cease, and an era of prosperity and good will flourished. While all of this, too, seemed almost miraculous, additional trappings insured that it continued. One of them, a significant military build up seemed incongruous with the times of peace, although war loomed on the horizon. The Triparteum granted the Chancellor unprecedented executive powers. His word suddenly became law, but due to his benevolence no one was concerned. Even with all of these things going on in the background, on the surface everything seemed just fine. Then it began. In the back rooms, led by the Chancellor, the council declared a secret holy war on the followers of Jesus, the Liberator.

It started with the cancellation of the tax exempt status for any religious assembly not associated with the Tri-World Church. Simultaneously, any member of the Tri-World Church received tax breaks on sales, income, and property taxes. Of course, a mandatory deduction from each paycheck supported the local expressions of the Tri-World Church. It then moved into subtle ways to expand the taxation of the dissidents.: a "Luxury Tax," levied on the luxury of not being associated with or licensed by the Tri-World Church; increased taxes on utilities, fuel, food, etc. avoided by a Tri-World Church member's special credit card. Further taxes were incurred for using cash or any other form of payment for services. the taxes were added during the transaction It finally came to open warfare, a military crack-down on the operations of the dissident assemblies.

Chapter 15 - The Soldier, Gomed

...And there will come a day when the soldier formed for the darkness will be reforged as a weapon for the Light...and the balance will be restored.

from the "Book of the Prophecies"

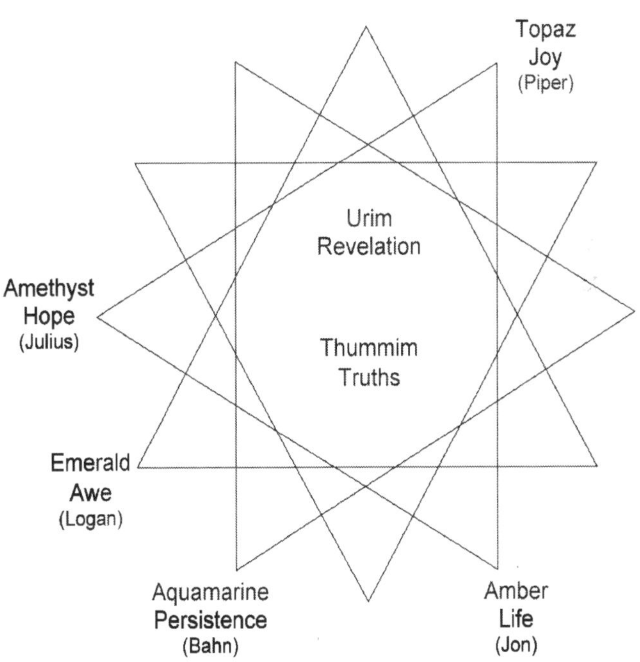

Gomed Akkub, a fiercely insidious warrior, joined the military to fight injustice and had been trained to do just that. He trained in a variety of mixed martial art forms of hand to hand and weapons combat. He excelled at them all, becoming particularly adept at stealth. If the Ninja still existed, he would have been a perfect candidate. As a Special Forces operative he had done tours all over the world and in all kinds of situations. In all of this he had not become simply a well-oiled fighting machine but a well-balanced human being. He knew when "restraint is the better side of valor." He exhibited controlled, yet passionate pursuit of excellence in all areas. If the Samurai still existed, he would have qualified as one of them also, knowing that martial arts were more art than martial. When the Triparteum formed the cream of the crop were conscripted to join their military arm. He nearly topped the list.

His additional studies focused more on honing the spirit than on conditioning the body, including introductions to the paranormal and the psychic sciences. Back in the 1500's, much of this would probably have been considered witchcraft. Every day, after specially designed physical training and the use of some initial meditative techniques, he received instruction in the forms of Qigong. These ancient Chinese exercises in breathing and movements, served to expand, focus, and express the Chi, the inner spirit-force. Few derived from these exercises more than an enhancement in speed and strength, save Gomed. His whole being seemed designed to channel and use this inner force. He could actually move some objects, seemed able to see around corners and developed an especially acute proximity sense. He could sense when someone focused on him just prior to an attack or the nearness of a threat. No one could sneak up on him or ambush him. All of these gifts, talents, skills and abilities made him perfectly suited for clandestine operations, and the Triparteum called on these skills often.

On one such operation he finally met his match. It had been described to him as a purely reconnaissance mission. He secretly deployed to a set of specific GPS coordinates to explore and investigate the area. He did so that very night. Wearing night vision optics that enhanced his vision to near daylight conditions, he arrived at the coordinates in the middle of a primeval forest. Suddenly something struck him from behind and only his finely honed senses and expert conditioning helped him avoid its major impact. He turned on his assailant to find nothing, save some slightly shimmering out-of-focus light. His opponent appeared invisible. He fought regardless. The fight lasted much longer than either combatant expected, but in the end Gomed collapsed on the forest floor, unconscious.

Battered and breathless himself, Zemir turned to Alathos, who stepped out of the thicket where he had been hiding.

"Now what am I supposed to do with him?" Zemir whispered.

They both received the same instructions. "Place him on Alathor's back, take him to the entrance, and deposit him inside."

Zemir quickly contested, "But he works for the enemy!"

The voice countered, "He does no longer." And so they obeyed.

Chapter 16 - A New Soldier

And there were seven archangels Gabriel, Michael, Rapheal, Raziel, Haniel, R'gel, and Uriel (also called Lucifer). Before the beginning of time, when the sons of God joined the choir of the stars and Uriel, the greatest among them, led them in worship, a special weapon was crafted for each of them, a sword that joined them in song.

from the "Chronicles of the Elohim"

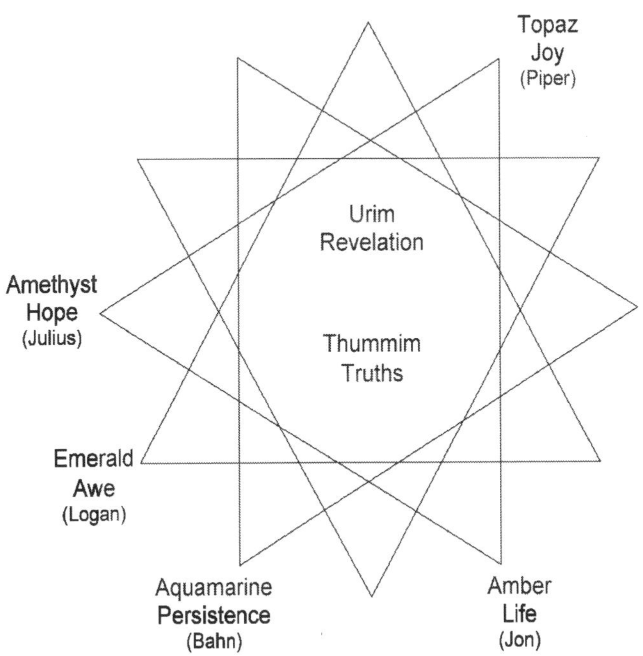

Bruised, battered, and bleeding, the soldier lay on the forested floor. The next morning he awoke in the arms of, not a priest, but, a simple, smiling gardener. His wounds had been cleansed, salved, and bandaged. He fell asleep once again and his dreams became less restless and tormented. He awoke to the smell of cooking. Before him sat a meager but delicious meal and a cup of sparkling, cold water. He savored each bite and felt its nourishment revitalizing both body and spirit. After completing his toilet, donning a robe, and taking advantage of the staff left for him, he stumbled haltingly out of the cottage and into a vast, immaculate garden. A small statue of indeterminate age, its features marred beyond recognition, graced the middle of the garden. A spring fed pool surrounded it and behind stood a small pavilion. The soldier stopped at the pool, knelt, bowed reverently to the statue, and took a drink from the spring using a small cup stored there obviously for that purpose. He rose and continued to the pavilion. He opened the screen door, astonished at how large it seemed on the inside. The middle of pavilion contained a small circular stone wall, as tall as a short sword, encompassing another small garden of herbs and a single tree, the height of a man. As he neared the wall, he noticed a kneeling pad at its base. Slowly, painfully, reverently, he knelt at the wall, laying the staff beside him. He bowed and rested his elbows on the wall into two grooves left there from the many who have prayed before him. When he raised his head, he discovered that an old man now sat beside him and he looked into a pair of eyes that seemed to see into his very soul. The soldier changed his position to match that of the old man.

The old man spoke, "This is not a place of war, but a place of peace. You have been brought here for a purpose, many purposes really. You must unlearn much. As a cup full of vinegar cannot be filled with sweet wine until it is emptied you must empty yourself in order to be refilled. You trained from your youth to be a warrior. You will become one again but with different skills, weapons, and fighting for a new cause. Are you ready to be empty? I will leave you to the Tree."

The old man rose from his sitting position, stood, and walked away with the grace of a leopard. The soldier remained seated, confused, puzzled over the old man's words.

"Gomed," a voice called his name. He turned around and faced the small garden once again, but no one was there. "Gomed," He heard it again, a voice both a whisper and a thunderous roar. Now he felt even more confused, and then slowly a deep peace began to invade his soul. He felt overcome with it, undone by it. The Tree spoke again, "Once I had to be a burning bush to arrest the attention of a shepherd, but this is a different time and a different place. Welcome to my place, the Sanctuary. Few who come here ever leave the same." Could the Tree really be talking to him? The blows he received to his head must have done more damage than he realized. He was either hallucinating, dreaming, or at least imagining this whole encounter, an encounter with the unbelievable, a talking tree.

"Your name shall become Meshar, for peace will be your weapon and with it you will disarm both fear and dismay. As my friend asked of you, are you ready to empty yourself that I may refill you?"

"Am I really talking to a tree or just dreaming all of this?" replied the soldier.

"I am much more than a tree, just as you are much more than a simple soldier. You may call me, Ha, ha, ha, ha.....," answered the Tree.

"Your name is Laughter?" questioned Meshar.

"While my names are many and I am the Son of Chayeem, you may simply call me Chayeem, for my father and I are one," continued the Tree. "Please remove your robe and let me look at you." Meshar removed his robe and that simple act of obedience completely healed all of his wounds, both inside and out. "Now we will begin your retraining," said the Tree, with laughter in his voice once again.

The next few weeks brought arduous joy. Much of this he thought he had learned as a child, the steps, the moves, the katas; but here he discovered a new harmony of body, soul, and spirit the likes of which he had not known. He mastered the staff, the bow and arrow, and the wooden sword, sparring with the old man, who surely did not seem very old when he had a staff or a wooden sword in his hand. Then one day the old man presented him with a sword more wonderful than he had ever seen. He marveled at its beauty and craftsmanship beyond peer and when he swung it, it sang in his hand. He remembered hearing the legends of the singing swords, forged of the stars, each with its own song made for one hand alone. This one seemed to be made for his. The old man had one and it seemed to be the complement to Meshar's, for when they sparred together the two swords sang in a harmony beautiful to hear and behold. Meshar's sword seemed to have a mind of its own. Sometimes when they sang together, the large olive green peridot that adorned its hilt pulsated in response to his movements and the songs they sang.

One day, as he neared the pavilion, the old man met him with a different staff in his hand. He held the crooked staff of a shepherd, and they left the compound for the first time. Until now his life had centered around the pavilion and the old man, unlearning his old fighting skills and learning these new ones that had culminated in the singing sword. But on this day all of that changed. The old man ushered him through a forest to green hills dotted with sheep. The old man began to teach him all about these silly little creatures with little sense, great curiosity, and a propensity towards getting lost. He also taught him to sing without his sword, wondrous new songs. They were songs of worship to the God of all things and especially to the Tree. He had begun to think that the two of them were somehow related, God and the Tree, but he still was not sure. Soon he composed his own songs under the starlit skies as the sheep lay sleeping. This continue for some time until the day the old man showed up and announced that the Tree would like to speak to him.

He entered the pavilion reverently, knelt and prayed at the small stone wall. When he finished, Chayeem spoke to him. "I have been very pleased with your progress, Meshar. I think you are ready for the next phase of your training." Suddenly the old man stood at his side carrying the singing sword. "If you will look closely at the jewel encased in the hilt of the sword, you will notice that the fitting that contains it unscrews," Chayeem said rather melodically. Meshar had thought that might be the case, but he had never tampered with the sword. "Please remove the fitting and drop the jewel into your hand," the Tree requested. Meshar complied, and when the jewel hit his palm liquid fire enveloped his soul and a powerful peace overwhelmed him. "This is the Meshar. Its name is the same as yours," the Tree continued. "This will become your most powerful weapon." Meshar smiled as he now held the Meshar and felt fully complete for the first time in his life. He had finally come home.

Chapter 17 - Out of the Meteor

And Jesus said to them, "I saw Satan and his angels fall like lightning from heaven."

And another sign appeared in the heavens. It was a great red dragon, with seven heads and ten horns, and on his heads were seven crowns. With his tail he swept down a third of the stars of heaven and led them to the earth.

Luke 10:18 & Revelation 12:3-4

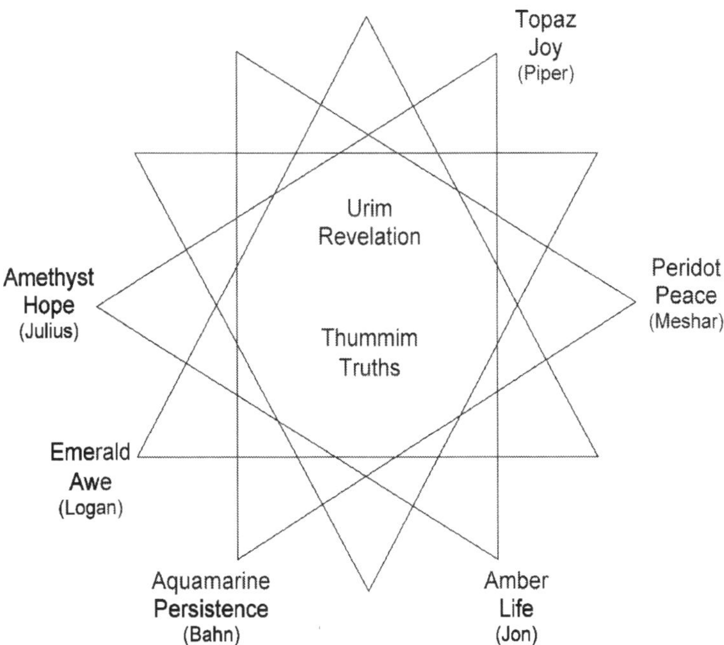

The origin of this stone differed from the others. Not a stone of antiquity hidden for millennia only to one day be revealed, quite the contrary, one of the leading scientific geniuses of the day developed it in a laboratory. Dr. Gideon Anakim had won the Nobel prize for his discovery of Lucidium. His work with new and exotic materials was unparalleled during the current regime of the Triparteum. His discoveries accounted for many of the recent breakthroughs in computing, bioelectronics, and genetic restructuring.

The unusual raw material for this stone came from a fallen star. One might call it one of the Nephilim (the Fallen Ones) spoken of old. Regardless, he recovered the material in a recently fallen meteorite. That material superseded all of his other discoveries, for in the meteor he found a vein of substance, likely a variation on pink tourmaline. He called it gideonite.

As a scientific community, they had been on the verge of artificial intelligence for years, but never discovered a material compact enough that could also conduct information fast enough to make AI truly feasible. Now they had gideonite. Similarly, they had stood on the brink of the discovery of artificial life, having all of the constituent parts discovered and understood. Yet they had been unable to create and sustain life artificially. Again, now they had gideonite. Though neither organic nor biological, it had the ability to link with both organic and biological materials. Gideonite contained astronomical raw processing power, and it could be easily empowered bioelectronically. Suddenly, Dr. Anakim found himself with tools to create both artificial intelligence and artificial life, and he worked diligently to make happen. He had fashioned his single source of extraterrestrial gideonite initially into a gem nearly 33mm across, at a weight of 500 carats. He approached the Triparteum for his next level of funding.

Adrian Quick held the Director of the Science Board position. He had once himself been a pioneer in microelectronics and was fully conversant with Gideon's work in bionics. Before leaving the private sector to direct this board for the chancellor, he had completed his own ground-breaking discoveries. While perhaps not as important as gideonite promised to be, Adrian's work had led to the development of the bionic microchip, Quicksilver, that could contain all of an individual's personal, medical, and financial information. The chip, when implanted in the back of a person's hand near the wrist, proved virtually indestructible and could be used for all purposes of buying and selling. Quicksilver's popularity soared, and beside yielding billions to Adrian's company, revolutionized the retail, medical, and financial industries. Some users adopted it so zealously that they implanted the chip in a tattoo of the company's logo on their foreheads. Its other most popular function, a Global Positioning Satellite (GPS) function, could track an individual to within inches of their actual location. This feature made it a runaway best seller for use with children. When a child turned 18 they had the option of no longer allowing their parents access to the data, but many forgot to turn it off. You could also give access to your GPS data to others via social media and revoke it if necessary. The chip was virtually impossible to remove, short of cutting off your hand. The GPS function of the chip continued to be secretly available to law enforcement and the security services of the Tripartuem even when access to its data had been revoked from all others.

Adrian and Gideon met in Adrian's somewhat spartan Director's office. He eschewed showmanship, but was laser-focused on efficiency and effectiveness. After sharing pleasantries and a glass of iced tea, they got down to business.

Adrian said, "Gideon, I am very interested in what you hope to accomplish with your next grant."

"Yes, I am astonished at the properties of gideonite, but I only have a small quantity of it. I want to explore the possibility of producing it synthetically."

"That could have unimaginable effects on society as we know it," Adrian continued. "Before we agree to finance that research, there are two things that the chancellor would like you to do for him as a special favor."

A bit taken aback, Gideon replied, "You have but to ask and I will do all in my power to make it happen."

Adrian smiled, "The chancellor has a friend that recently died of a brain aneurysm. She has been cryogenically preserved and we believe that you can use a small portion of the gideonite to restore her brain functions and bring her back to life."

Gideon smiled in return. "To raise the dead would indeed be a feather in the chancellor's hat."

Adrian's smile dimmed, "This project will be totally secret and never revealed to the public or private sectors. It will simply be done as a favor to the chancellor."

Gideon grimaced, "I'm sorry, I meant no disrespect."

"None taken," soothed Adrian.

"And the second thing?" Gideon prompted hesitantly.

"Hmmm, let's complete the first assignment before we start on the second one. Oh, and Gideon, there is no financial ceiling on your spending to accomplish this. Just let me know what resources you need."

Gideon left the Director's office with his mind going a million miles an hour in multiple directions. Revolutionary, if he could truly pull it off, and he felt confident that he could. Gideon did not know the true reason behind the chancellor's request. The fictitious chancellor's friend had actually been the wife of the leader of a small dissident religious sect that the Triparteum had watched for some time. Their close surveillance of the sect ensured that, when the wife, Mary, died, the authorities had been notified and her body intercepted while in transit to the university to be designated for scientific study. Now, indeed, she would be part of a scientific study. If her resurrection succeeded, she would be given "miraculously" back to the leader of the sect and become an implanted GPS to their movements 24/7.

The surgery had been a total technical success and looked especially promising on their first human subject. He labored under enormous emotional pressure to succeed since he believed Mary had been a personal friend of the chancellor, but Dr. Anakim did his best work under pressure. One of his famous quotes was, "I don't worry about external pressure, I create my own eustress to motivate my top performance at all times." His record of achievements demonstrated how well that worked for him. It had taken less than a quarter of the gideonite to create the network to reunify the portion of Mary's brain damaged by the aneurysm, and it seemed potentially possible that she would awake with full use of all her functions, physical, mental, and emotional. The brain can live about 8 minutes without oxygen, and she had been quick-frozen almost immediately with everything but the damaged area intact. He readied all the external life support systems for the moment she was quick-thawed, and performed most of the surgery while she lay still in a frozen state. The gideonite amazingly allowed them to keep her in an unconscious state even after they revived her. The entire time of her rehabilitation, she performed as though in a hypnotic trance. She remained fully awake, not comatose, she just did not know it. For Mary, it would have seemed like she simply went to sleep the day she died and woke up the next day when her consciousness returned to her.

"Good morning, Mary, I am Dr. Gideon Anakim. How are you feeling?" Gideon asked.

"I'm feeling just fine, thank you. When can I go home?" she replied.

"Well, we would like you to remain with us a few days just to assure all of us that everything is working perfectly," he answered.

Then he told her about the aneurysm and her brain surgery. They intentionally remained vague on the timing and specifics and she did not really care because it seemed like she had fallen asleep in the midst of all that pain and woken up the next day just fine. From her point of view she had received a miracle. She wanted to call her husband, but they kept her in a totally restricted area, with no cell phone reception and no communication with the outside world. The delicate nature of what they had done and were doing required it. She supposed she should have asked more questions, but she felt grateful to be alive. And then they brought her home to the farm.

Shortly after Mary's release, Gideon met again with Adrian Click. A secretary ushered him into Adrian's office to another warm reception.

"Gideon, my friend. It's so good to see you. I hear that you have been totally successful with the chancellor's first request," he said, smiling widely.

"Yes!" replied Gideon, "We have had near miraculous results with the procedure. The chancellor's friend, Mary, feels like she simply fell asleep amidst all of her aneurysm's pain and awoke the next day fully healed!"

"Wonderful, wonderful," Adrian chuckled. "So, are you ready for the chancellor's next request?"

"Certainly, what is his next challenge for me?" Gideon replied brimming with confidence.

"Come," invited Adrian as he arose from his chair. "The team awaits us in the conference room."

Chapter 18 - Resurrection

...And evil will be reversed and become live again, but whose purpose will this duplicity serve?

from the "Book of the Prophecies"

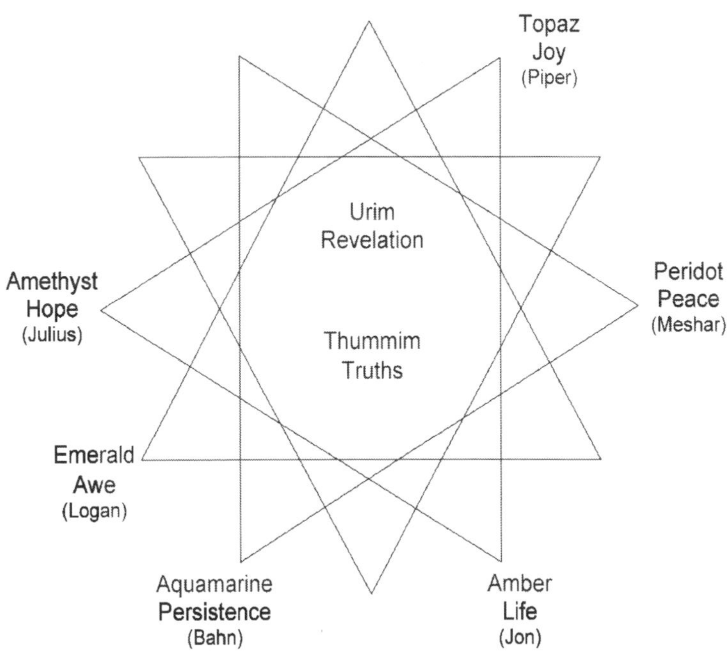

He heard a knock at the door. "How odd," Jon thought. "Who would knock? This is the farm. Everyone is welcome here. The door is never locked." He walked out of the kitchen, down the long hallway to the entryway, opened the door, and stepped back. It seemed like someone punched him in the solar plexus. He could not catch his breath nor believe his eyes, but there she stood, his wife, his dead wife.

"Mary, is it really you?" asked Jon.

"Yes Jon, I'm pretty sure it's me," laughed Mary.

"But you died of a brain aneurysm. I was there. I saw you die!" He was afraid.

Afraid she was not real, afraid to find it just a trick, an illusion. Yet there she stood in all of her regal beauty. She walked over to him slowly. He stood transfixed, wavering between fear and amazement. He struggled to believe and yet feared deception. She reached out her hand no longer laughing but with tears glistening in her eyes touched his cheek. He shied away. Would her touch be cold and clammy or unreal in some other way? He still loved her deeply, for love does not end at the grave. She trembled not understanding his withdrawal. She too was frightened. He shuddered as she finally did touch him. He couldn't hold himself back any longer. He took a step and clasped her to his chest as the tears came in a rushing torrent. They cried together holding each other tightly. He explored her touch by touch, all the old familiar places remained there. To his amazement she did the same to him. The tears marked the beginning of the end of frustration, the opening of a doorway to joy. They embraced slowly and then passionately. She stepped back, took his hand, and led him to the living room. He went reluctantly, still afraid, but with an increasing joy. They sat on the couch. He cradled her head against his shoulder. Now it felt as though they had been parted only days ago. How would he fill in the gap? How would he make up for all this lost time? He pondered these questions, but she spoke, and he played the role of a good listener.

"It was like they flipped a switch and I woke up in a hospital. Well, at least I thought it was a hospital. I later found out it was an experimental laboratory." She continued, "I seemed just fine. I was weak, tired, but otherwise felt just fine. I remembered having a terrible headache at home and then everything was black and blank until the moment I had woke up." I asked the staff, "Where am I?"

The only response I got was, "It's OK. You are OK now. You are safe. The doctor will be with you shortly."

I was thirsty and ravenously hungry. I asked them for something to eat and drink and they brought me both. The doctor showed up soon after that. He was tall and seemed almost regal. Perhaps it was his confidence or maybe he was just so comfortable in his skin that he came across as regal.

"Let me introduce myself, Mary. I am Dr. Gideon Anakim, and you are a patient here at my clinic. I know you have many questions and I will answer as many as I can."

"Jon, you know that I am a pretty good judge of character and I instantly found myself trusting him. He told me about the aneurysm and how they had operated on me. The brain surgery he had performed, leading his team, saving my life, it was like a miracle, because when I regained consciousness I was just fine. I didn't need any rehabilitation or therapy. I had lost none of my memory, motor skills, or anything. It was amazing. That was just a few days ago. I wanted to call you and let you know I was OK, but they said that the sensitive nature of all the equipment there didn't allow the use of cell phones and there were no landlines to the outside of the facility. They convinced me that a surprise would be more fun. So, they brought me to the farm and dropped me off just now. I'm sorry for the shock. I didn't even realize that I had been dead, or that you thought I was."

"Do you have any idea how long you have been dead?" he blurted out.

She shook her head, "No?"

He felt all the old grief was returning. He stopped, took a few deep breaths, and continued. "I'm sorry! It's still quite a shock." He smiled, "It is nice to have you back."

All the residents of the farm had lots of questions for most of which she had no answers. She did not know the location of the facility or anything about it. She knew only Dr. Anakim's name and the few answers he had given to her too few questions. As the community continued to talk and pray about the situation over the next few days, they all agreed that something wrong lay at the very foundation of the whole thing. Why had they deceived Jon and let him believe Mary died? Why had they not kept him informed about everything? The entire event smelled like the scheming of the Triparteum regime.

Then one evening as they lay in bed she whispered, "I think they want me to betray you! I'm not sure how or why, but there is this nagging falsehood lingering in my mind." Jon thought that perhaps many layers of truth lay hidden in Mary's simple statement. Maybe she truly harbored a thinly disguised mistrust for the doctor she had so instantly trusted, and it seemed almost as though she had been brainwashed, hypnotized, or something similar that had left her with a series of subliminal suggestions. At least she had not become one of the Triparteum itself. Either that or else she played her part with an element of greatness that only a professional actress could pull off. How could this be? Would he never be able to fully trust his own wife again? Was she now a tool in the hands of his enemy?

PART 6

THE ARK OF GOD

Chapter 19 - Finding the Ark

The records show that the prophet Jeremiah, in response to a divine message, gave orders that the Tent of Meeting (the Tabernacle) and the Ark of the Covenant should go with him. He traveled until he reached the top of the mountain from which Moses had seen God's promised land. There Jeremiah found a cave. He carried in the Tabernacle , the Ark, and the Altar of Incense, into the cave and laid them there. He then blocked up the entrance to the cave.

2 Maccabees 2:4-5

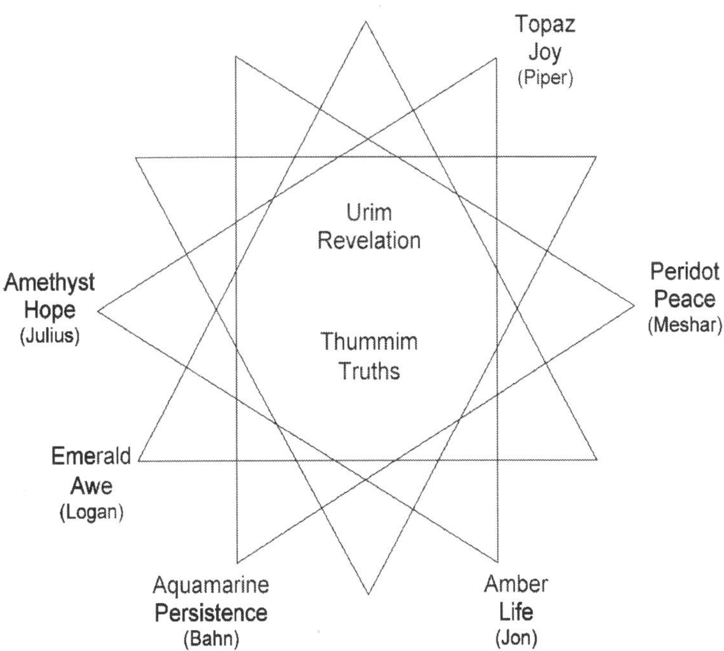

Strange, how miraculous things begin with ordinary, everyday incidences, such as digging a basement. Building a new meeting house would have been easier, but they decided on a large meeting room in the basement instead, it meant less taxes. Without visible changes to the exterior of the farm, the powers that be would assume nothing had change. That sounded dishonest, but could they be honest with a corrupt, unjust, and discriminatory government? The State ignored bona fide members of the state church who kept up on your dues and taxes, but any who for reason of conscience could not or did not, fell under suspicion. Local officials seemed to invent ways to investigate and harass those individuals. Since they had withdrawn from the state church and had been listed as belonging to a group of dissenters, varying representatives of the State frequently visited them, all intent on investigating some manner of false allegation. First the health department came up periodically to inspect the water in their well. Allegedly the state worried that their water supply might be adversely affected by local groundwater, or perhaps contained contaminates usually filtered out by the State treatment plants. The State had already created a special tax for those people who had their own wells. Their group, in turn, feared that the state might contaminate the well water to force them into using the state's water supply, but if they tried, they never succeeded. Fortunately one of their members had trained as a lab technician, for he discovered the one time the government attempted to falsify a water test to say that it contained some pollutant. The State's means of correcting the situation would have been to add a little something to the water. As to just exactly what kind of chemical it would have been, he have no idea. Rumors claimed that the State had a number of drugs on hand designed to reduce the "rebellious impulse," as they called it. They had many visitors besides the health department, property tax officials, utilities department, to name a few. Not that they were getting paranoid about the situation, but neither did the wish to give the State another reason to come out, look them over, and invent another tax. That they remained virtually self-supporting also heightened the State's suspicions. In fact, the only reason any of them needed to work part time was to keep informed of all the taxes. And they expected the persecution to intensify. Some day someone would create a law that made raising personal food unlawful for health and safety reasons or a law that required dependency on the state in certain areas, whatever those areas might be.

That's explained Jon's presence down below their farm house digging the basement when the wall gave way, and he found himself in a small underground tunnel. He would have gone back for a flashlight except he could see. A light red, pulsating glow appeared to originate just around the corner lit the tunnel. Having more courage than sense, he went to investigate. Around the corner the tunnel narrowed down to barely allow a man through. There, hanging from the roof of the tunnel and guarding the entrance to whatever lay beyond, appeared the largest ruby he had ever seen. It hung by a beautifully hand-worked chain, encased in a setting of the same craftsmanship. Apparently, the tremor of the cave-in had set it in motion, so now it slowly spun on the chain, and the light that originated from it created the pulsing effect. It slowed and finally stopped facing Jon. He felt as though an eye watched, probing the depths of his soul, measuring him. The walls of the tunnel seemed to close in, and he became increasingly aware of the weight of dirt above him. What if, suddenly, it should all collapse? As his fear grew he prayed, not in words actually, but more in feelings and impressions. He faced his fear, and soon it passed through him. Perhaps he had passed a test for the light of the gem increased, and he received a second washing of fear. As the light increased, a flaw or mark on the gem became visible. Like the visible star on a star sapphire, so a star became visible on this ruby; the Star of David.

Why should the Star of David strike terror to his soul? Jon recalled that much of his upbringing had tended to be on the religiously legalistic side, with some superstitious overtones. He remembered being told quite distinctly that the traditional Star of David should not be called the Star of David, but the Star of Solomon, one of the most powerful symbols in witchcraft. All witchcraft of any consequence began with the Star of Solomon. Jon took at least one step backwards instinctively, then paused to reflect, "Is not the false often a distortion or a bending of the truth?" Finally, this terror, too, passed through him. Jon felt light and pure as if some purging had just taken place at deeper than a physical level. Jon advanced upon the gem, reached up and unhooked it from the roof of the tunnel and unhesitatingly placed it carefully over his head. It was warm, seemed almost alive. Jon feared that touching it with his dirty hands might somehow mar or defile it.

In front of Jon the tunnel opened to a larger cavern. In the midst of the cavern lay something the shape of a large box. It seemed encased or encrusted with the sediments of the cavern, and at each end stood a tall pole-like structure. It seemed as though time and space stood still. The silence echoed, and a sharp pain increased in his chest. As he looked down at the still radiating jewel, Jon realized he had quit breathing. It seemed a sacrilege to do so now. The whole atmosphere seemed pregnant with a purity and holiness that not only took his breath away but seemed reluctant to give it back. The pain became unendurable, and he finally broke the spell and inhaled. The light from the ruby changed to a deep shade of purple and the box with its poles began to glow like white objects seen under black light. Jon stood in awe as he realized what lay before him. Although he was puzzled by the lack of the Cherubim, one at each end of the box, he felt certain that he had just discovered the lost Ark of the Covenant. He fell to his knees, engulfed in awe. Finally he stood and reverently retraced his steps, hung the pendant back on its hook and left the tunnel. He went upstairs, got a blanket, and covered the hole in the wall.

Chapter 20 - Anna and the Way

I am the way, the truth, and the life; no one will complete their journey to the Father without Me...

John 14:1

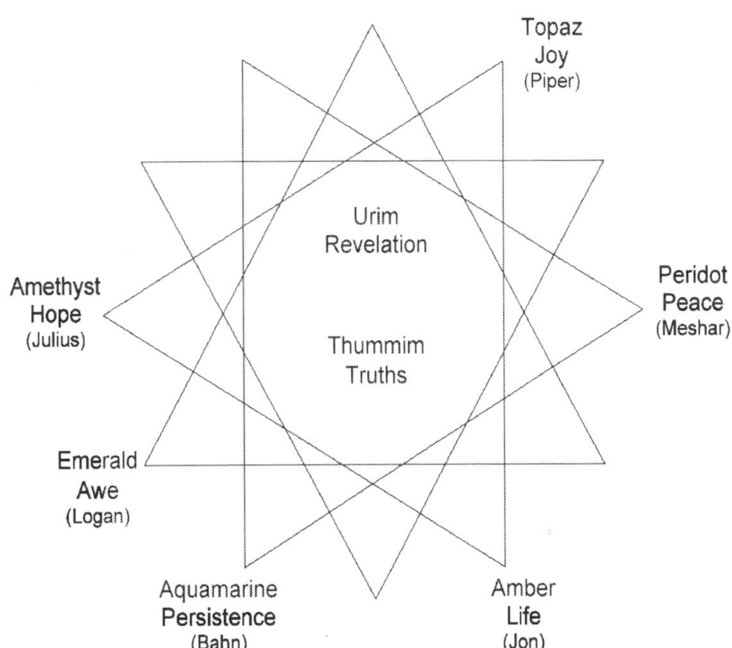

Youth group met Saturday nights in the basement and included Anna. After some fun activities Jon gave a message. His topic that night was titled "Things Are Not Always What They Seem." Afterwards, one of the kids asked him about the blanket on the wall. He passed it off with a joke and they all headed upstairs, except Anna. Jon came back down moments later to find her standing before the blanket.

She had her hand on it, "What's behind the blanket, pastor?" she asked.

Without realizing it, he replied, "Would you like to see?"

She laughed, "Don't forget, I'm blind."

Jon quickly countered, "Oh, I'm sorry. It's a cavern. I can take you in, though, if you'd like."

She replied, "Yes, I'd like that."

Jon moved the blanket aside, took her hand, and they walked into the cavern by the light of the stone. Anna stopped, the shining stone hanging just above her head. She reached up and touched it and it blazed with light. Jon took a step back in shock and awe. Then he stepped forward, unhooked the delicate chain that surrounded the stone, and placed it over Anna's head. The stone rested next to her heart.

She slowly turned in a circle and spoke, "Pastor Jon, this is the Way stone. With it He will show us the way," she paused, visibly shaken, and continued in a whisper, "With it I can see, not with my eyes, but with my heart. I can see, Pastor Jon, I can see," as tears coursed down her cheeks...and his too.

Chapter 21 - Within the Ark

...And when they discover My Ark, its new contents will be revealed for it is the dawn of a new age...

from a "Maccabean Fragment"

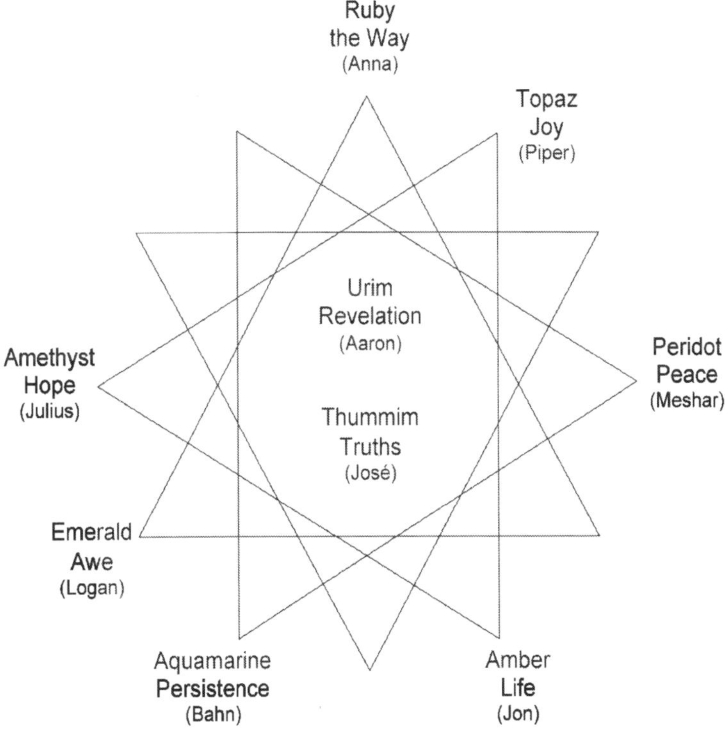

The three of them, José, Aaron, and José's dog Adrian journeyed the entire day and into the evening. They stopped only to eat their light lunches, to drink some water outside of a couple of service stations and once at a park. They had no supper that evening, so by the time they found the farm they were tired and hungry. Jon welcomed them with open arms. Jon welcomed everyone with open arms especially dogs. In fact, Adrian was the first to arrive, having run on ahead of the other two. While Jon sat on the veranda, reading in the cool of the evening, he spied a dog running down their road. "That looks like Adrian, José's dog," he thought to himself as it bounded up onto the deck. His startled, "Adrian, is that you?" resulted in a a pair of paws in his lap, the dog's tongue licking his face, and a wildly wagging tail. "Good to see you, old boy! Where's José?" he asked. Adrian dropped down out of his lap and turned to face the road.

As José and Aaron turned the corner and the farm house came into view, they both quickened their pace. Jon waved from the lighted porch, and they waved back in the light of the streetlamp that marked that turn in the road.

Jon came down the steps to greet them, smiling broadly. "So good to see you José," he spoke as he wrapped him in an embrace. "And this is?"

"Jon, this is my new friend Aaron. You are going to like him!"

Jon shook Aaron's hand. "A pleasure, I'm sure. Any friend of José is more than welcome here."

When they dropped hands, Aaron cocked his head slightly to one side and said matter of factly, "Your wife Mary has been returned to you!"

Jon could not have been more startled if Aaron had just slapped him in the face!

José questioned, "Mary? I thought Mary was dead!"

When Jon's wits returned he said, "How do you know my wife, and how could you possibly know she is here?"

Aaron bowed his head, "I'm sorry, that was a bit insensitive, but none the less true. I spoke presumptuously, please forgive me."

José broke in, "Aaron is a prophet among other things."

Jon shook his head, still trying to dispel the shock. "Have you had supper?" he asked.

"No," they said in chorus.

"Well, then come in and join us. I believe a few of us are still eating." As they mounted the steps to the porch,

José asked, "We passed some of the circus wagons on the way in, are they here?"

"Yes," responded Jon, "Some are having supper with us now."

As they opened the door and entered the house, the sounds of a joyful family at supper filled their ears and hearts. The large dining room used to be two rooms, but as their numbers grew, they had remodeled it into a single room. It also doubled as their meeting room when they all assembled for worship, prayer, and sharing. An assortment of people gathered around the dining room table in varying stages of their evening meal.

Jon began the introductions with, "Many of you already know my dear friend, José. He will be staying with us for a while and has brought with him Aaron whom I'm sure you will all soon count as a friend also. Aaron, this is Julius, Logan, and Anna from the circus, along with Judy & Todd."

Mary entered the room from the kitchen and José quickly crossed the dining room to embrace her. "Mary, this is truly amazing. I thought we had lost you."

"Yes it is," she stammered. "I'll have to tell you about it later."

Aaron now joined them and extended his hand to her. "It is truly a pleasure to have you back from the dead," he said as he brought her hand to his lips and kissed it.

"I don't think we have met before, have we?" Her stammer continued.

"No, my Lady, we have not, but I know you regardless." His penetrating gaze held hers and for some unknown reason spoke peace and wholeness to her heart and mind.

She smiled, "I'll get you both some dishes." She departed back into the kitchen. Although new to their group, Aaron fit in seamlessly and soon all re-entered the joyful revelry that the two of them had interrupted.

With the meal completed and most of the dishes cleared from the table, they began a more serious discussion over their tea. Jon, as their pastor, led in this. "The culture around us is becoming increasingly hostile to followers of the Liberator. We have all been planning and praying about our next steps. José and Aaron, I would like to show you our most recent discovery. You can leave your tea here. We shouldn't be long." A chorus of chairs scraped on the hardwood floor as they slid back from the table. All rose and followed Jon down into the basement. "We were looking to expand this room and make it another meeting room when part of the dirt wall gave way to reveal something interesting." He pulled back the blanket covering the entryway into the cavern. The hole had been enlarged and fortified with a cross-beam and supports. They had also widened and added some supporting structures inside the cavern itself, along with some artificial lighting. The group entered two abreast: Jon and Julius, José and Aaron, Logan and Anna, Judy and Todd. Mary had stayed upstairs to take care of the supper dishes.

As they rounded the corner, the cavern deepened, widened, and expanded. They fanned out in a semi-circle around the object in the middle of the cavern, a box-like structure encased in the cavern sediment.

Aaron dropped immediately to his knees to exclaim, "Do you have any idea what this is?"

Jon whispered, “I would appreciate your assessment.”

Pointing to the poles extending from the object Aaron continued, “That is the Ark of the Covenant!”

Jon countered, “I had that impression too, but where are the two cherubs that cover the mercy seat?”

At this point Anna stepped forward, the red Way stone glowing through her light blouse, “They are both here, in person!” she said as the two angels appeared.

Suddenly they were all kneeling, not in reverence to the angels, but to the Ark of God. Two angelic voices spoke in harmony. “Aaron and the one called The Saint, you have been called here to restore the Ark to its glory.” The moment passed. It seemed as though fresh air poured into the room. They all took a deep breath and stood up in near unison, quietly turning and finding their way out of the chamber.

On their way out José turned to Aaron, “I was simply looking for sanctuary, but I think we have found much more than that.”

When José said the word “Sanctuary,” Aaron stumbled and nearly collapsed. He stopped, calmed himself, looked back over his shoulder into the chamber and replied. “Yes, much more.”

The next morning after breakfast and prayer they began to discuss their approach to removing the sediment from the Ark.

“No one is supposed to touch the Ark. Uzzah died when he did,” recalled José from the Old Testament scriptures.

“That is right, but then why would the angels say we are called to restore it?” countered Aaron.

Jon added, “Maybe there is a way to remove the sediment without touching the Ark?”

José remembered, “Hey, I think the Ark was covered in the veil when it was transported? Perhaps it still is. Then whatever we do to remove the sediment would only involve touching the veil.”

Jon continued “That would be true if the veil has survived all these years. Shouldn’t it have rotted away by now? It was just normal material was it not?”

Aaron chimed in, “Yes, I believe there was nothing special about it except that it was consecrated. And yet the clothes of the

Israelites while they were wandering in the wilderness were just plain clothes too, but they didn't ever wear out for those forty plus years. Maybe we should just ask Him specifically?" Aaron didn't even bow his head. He rarely did. He just said, "God, how would you like us to remove the sediment from Your Ark?"

"Wow! That was easy," exclaimed José, "I immediately saw a picture of a hammer and concrete chisel. Jon, do you have some in the tool shed?"

Off they went, found the tools and proceeded back to the cavern chamber. Aaron spoke or prayed, it was hard to tell with him, "Who should strike the first blow?"

Anna had just walked into the chamber behind them. They all turned in unison and asked, "Anna?"

She replied with a simple "Yes?"

Aaron spoke again. "I have in my hand a concrete chisel and a hammer. We think you are supposed to strike the first blow to remove the sediment from the Ark."

"OK." she replied simply. Jon handed her the tools and directed her hand to the Ark.

Jon thought, "They do remember that she is blind, don't they?"

Anna moved the chisel around some until it seemed that it rested in the center of the top of the Ark. She brought the hammer back and gave it a little tap. The tap resounded like a thunder clap. All the sediment now resided on the cavern floor. The Ark stood there covered in nothing but the veil.

"What next?" Aaron asked. "We may remove the veil," he added. "José, you take that end and I will take this one." He motioned José to the opposite end of the box. They took the veil by its four corners. "On three, we will lift it slowly. One, two, three." Aaron and José proceeded to slowly lift the veil off of the box to reveal the Ark. Even in the artificial light the golden box blazed like the sun. Aaron and José took two steps to the right, turned their backs to the Ark, and proceeded to fold up the veil between them. They handed it to Jon and turned to face the box again. The angels, now revealed in their full glory, sheathed their flaming swords and moved to stand at each end of the Ark. They stretched their wings out in front of them, over the Ark to meet in the middle, above the mercy seat.

Anna spoke up, "Ah, that's better. That's how I had pictured it." They all stood transfixed for a few moments then the angels folded their wings behind their backs again.

The first of the angels spoke, "I am Ayah and this is my twin Anan. We watch over the Ark. You may wish to hide your eyes for a moment as we remove the lid that you call the Mercy Seat." They all hid their eyes as the angels at each end grasped the lid and lifted it free from the rest of the box. Suddenly, it seemed as if the sun burst forth again, this time from inside of the box, and then the light returned to normal.

Anan spoke, "Aaron, you may now look into the box and tell the others what you see."

Reluctantly and reverently Aaron complied. "All I see is what appears as a large log, lying in the bottom of the Ark."

The angel continued, "Yes, because you live on the other side of His cross, the tablets of the Law have been removed. You live in a state of grace. Similarly, because He is the Bread of Life, the manna too has been removed."

"And the log?" asked Aaron.

"It is from the One Tree, Chayeem," and as he spoke the Tree's name, the air in the chamber seemed to reverberate melodically.

Ayah then spoke, "And is there a word inscribed on the Tree?"

Aaron replied, "Yes, the word Bakar, which in Hebrew means 'Open!" and with his speaking of the word the log split open as if cleaved with an axe to reveal two jewels.

Ayah spoke again, "The large diamond like jewel is much more than a diamond. It is the Urim. Aaron, you may remove it from its place in the Tree."

Aaron reached into the box, careful not to touch the sides, and removed the stone. As he did, light and revelation nearly overwhelmed him.

"José," spoke Anan, "You may step forward and remove the other stone, the Thummim."

José complied, and looking down into the box saw the largest and most amazing sapphire-like jewel he had ever imagined. Reverently he reached in, grasped the jewel, stood back up, and with it still clasped to his chest collapsed in a heap on the floor, under the weight of the truths the stone contained.

PART 7

THE FINAL STONES

Chapter 22 - Tanaheil

A three-strand chord is not easily broken nor the friendship of three companions.

from the "Proverbs of the Seer"

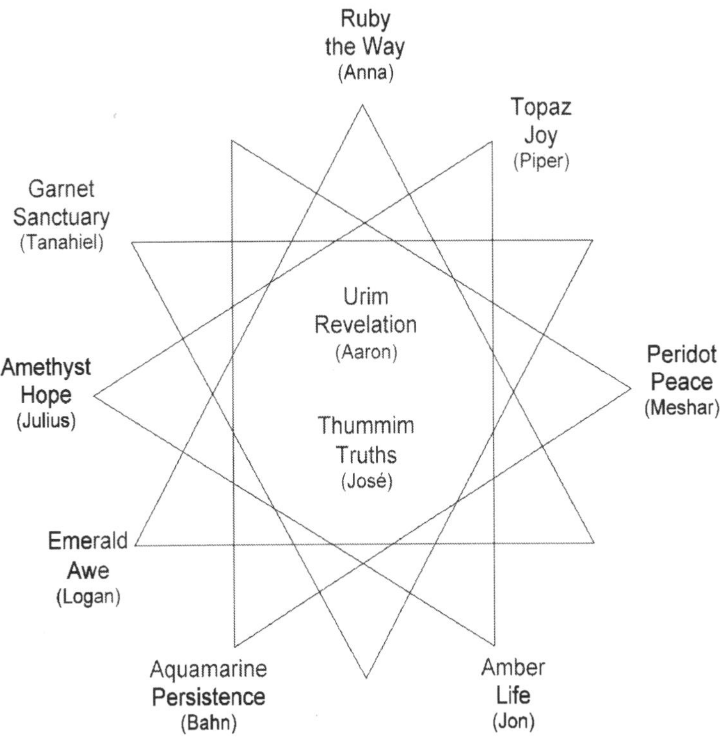

The Way stone initially had a sister stone, nearly its twin. While the Way stone resembled a large ruby, its sister stone was a deep red garnet. Unfortunately, it too had been lost to the rebellion after the choirmaster fell from his exalted position. Singing swords, sacred stones, so much was lost in the fall of the angels and the subsequent fall of mankind. Mankind believed that the fallen angels became the demons of earth and joined the enemy in the battle against good, but history does not tell a story of a battle between good and evil. It describes a war between life and anti-life. Where the Way stone exuded a kind of purity, its sister stone spoke of sanctity, a holiness deeper than simple purity. Purity deals with clarity. Sanctity speaks of a unique beauty that is set apart.

Tanahiel was beautifully unique from birth, in fact, even from before birth. Within the womb she seemed to somehow respond to worship and beauty by radiating a kind of warmth to her mother. She moved never sharply nor abruptly, but with purpose, measured, graceful, and fluid. While a young girl she excelled in ballet. As she grew, she learned Tai Chi, a martial art more art than martial. In school she befriended many, as she radiated a rare kind of serenity for one so young. She never seemed self conscious or self absorbed, but rather intentionally other-centered. While Anna, who came to possess the Way stone, considered her upbringing spiritually suppressive, Tanahiel experienced quite the opposite. She grew up in a spiritual culture of awe and wonder. Logan the dwarf became her other best friend, besides Anna, and it seemed providential that they all ended up at the circus.

Tanahiel had a special place, only a short walk from the circus grounds, a meadow and small creek guarded by a few elms and oaks. One sunny day she as lay in the meadow basking in the evening sun, the sun seemed to darken. She sat up with a start. A large eagle had landed in one of the oaks, and his form blocked the sun. He had something in his beak. He swooped to land in front of her, and for some reason she did not fear him. Logan stood beside her, holding Anna by the hand.

"How did they get here?" she mused. The huge bird took a step forward and held out the object. It looked like a plain linen purse.

"He wants you to have it," whispered Logan. "Reach out your hand."

She complied. The eagle dropped the purse into her hand. She thought he smiled, but then how does an eagle smile? He turned and flew off. She looked down at the purse in her hand, untied the drawstring, and opened it. She then poured its contents into her other hand, revealing a large, deep red garnet.

Anna looked toward the stone and, though she was blind, said, "I believe that is the Sanctuary stone." And she, Logan, and Tanahiel all smiled in wonder.

Chapter 23 - Todah

My angels are sent to minister to those who are to be saved and how will they minister, guard, aid, help, counsel, and intervene? Let me tell you.

from the "Ancient musings of the Wise"

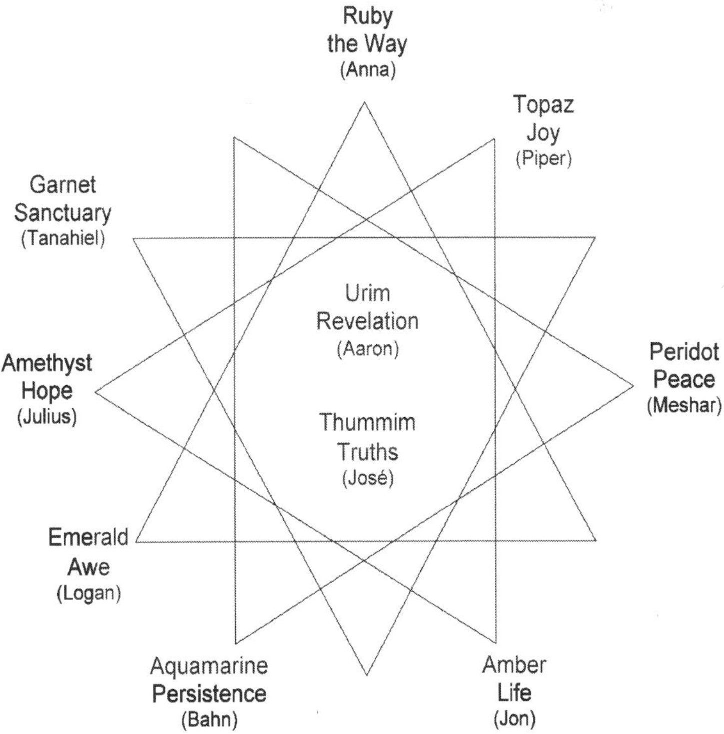

Nothing about her, at least from outward appearances, seemed to mark her as anything but plain and ordinary. In a crowd she would not only go unnoticed, she would be totally passed over completely, unseen. She had learned early that no one saw her, no one cared about her and, rather than responding in woundedness, she turned her attention to the rest of the world that was unseen, the spiritual. She developed an incredible relationship with her angel. Every person has one assigned to them though most of people do not know that. Perhaps they are not even supposed to know it. It might have been a breach of heavenly protocol for her angel to reveal himself to her, but she knew he was there long before he did reveal himself. She perceived things that clearly.

It might have had something to do with the closeness of their names. His was Teedhar, translated as oak, and hers, Todah meant thanksgiving. Whenever something wonderful happened to her she would exclaim, "Tadah!" She believed her delight increased when she shared it with him. Her enthusiasm led her to discover him in the first place. She had noticed some small wonder, like dew on a spider's web, a single flower in a gravel path, or something else seemingly insignificant, and when she responded with a "Tadah," she felt a slight disturbance in the atmosphere, like an involuntary spiritual chuckle. Others would not have noticed it, but she did. She looked around to find its origin and, seeing none, did not pass it off as her imagination but assumed something or someone stood there whom she could not see. Because she noticed the insignificant, she discovered him through little things: the way the light seemed to bend differently just outside of her normal vision, the small interruptions, the chance things that did or did not happen. All of these she began to assign to his guardianship. Eventually, she realized she often felt his presence. He seemed assigned to her, and she began to talk to him.

One day she finally asked him , "What is your name? If we are to be friends, it would be nice to know."

He should not have responded, but a beautiful picture of an oak tree suddenly captivated her mind.

"Oak? Your name is Oak?" she exclaimed.

He laughed. Later she looked "oak" up in the dictionary and figuring out he probably spoke the original tongue decided his name was "Teedhar." She called him Ted for short and he seemed pleased that she cared.

Early one morning she sat outside in the sun reading one of the early chapters in the Chronicles of the Elohim when she came across a passage she had never seen before. Right after God had made woman, "Clay had called her 'Dawn'"for she symbolized the start of everything new and fresh. She began all things "very good." One beautiful morning Dawn awoke at the edge of the garden as the sun broke over the hills and shown with its full force into the garden. Such breath-taking beauty caused Dawn to gasp in amazement and a single tear of sheer joy trickled down her cheek. She turned to share the beauty of the moment with Clay and turned right into a branch which scratched her cheek. The blood, now mixed with the tear of joy, ran down her chin and dropped onto the garden floor where it crystallized into a jewel of great beauty. Clay reached out, touched her cheek and healed the wound, then reached down and picked up the jewel. He looked for a place to put it, but he had no pockets. He wore no clothes, so he just held onto it for the rest of the morning. He planned to take it to the great tree Chayeem who stood in the middle of the garden and ask Him about it or ask God Himself later that afternoon. But circumstances with the other tree that stood in the center of the garden intervened, and he left the stone somewhere and never had a chance to retrieve it." She set the book down.

"Her blood filled tear had crystalized into a jewel. Was that even possible?" she thought. The book said it, so it must be true. "I wonder what ever happened to it," she mused.

She remembered one of her mother's favorite sayings, "You have not because you ask not," which she usually followed up with, "It is never wrong to ask. He will always answer. He may say 'Yes, no, or not yet!' but He will always answer." She felt that Teedhar sat at her side. She turned to her right and looked into his eyes, or where she assumed his eyes would be if he were nine feet tall but sitting next to her.

She asked, "Do you know what became of the jewel made from Dawn's tear?" The atmosphere suddenly became electric. She stood. Maybe she should have fallen on her face. The air to her right shimmered and seemed to hiss and sputter, although she heard no sound, and a portal opened between the realms. There he stood, closer to ten feet tall, awesome, terrifying, and beautiful, all rolled into one, but smiling like the dawn of something wonderful. His sword sang as he withdrew it. The music brought tears to her eyes, as the sword swung in a complete arc, swirled in his hand, and stopped with the hilt up and the blade straight down. He unscrewed the end of the hilt and offered it to her. She reached out her hand, trembling. He upended it and into her hand fell a light orange zircon.

His voice whispered and thundered between the realms at the same time, "The Dawn stone, one of the twelve. I have been keeping it for you since before you were born." The portal collapsed and she almost did too. She shudderingly took a deep breath and opened her hand to reveal the Dawn stone still there.

Chapter 24 - More Than a Dog

And the earth brought forth living creatures (literally souls), each after its own kind.

Genesis 1

When we cross the barrier between the species will we pollute their souls?

from the "British Scientific Journal of Genetics"

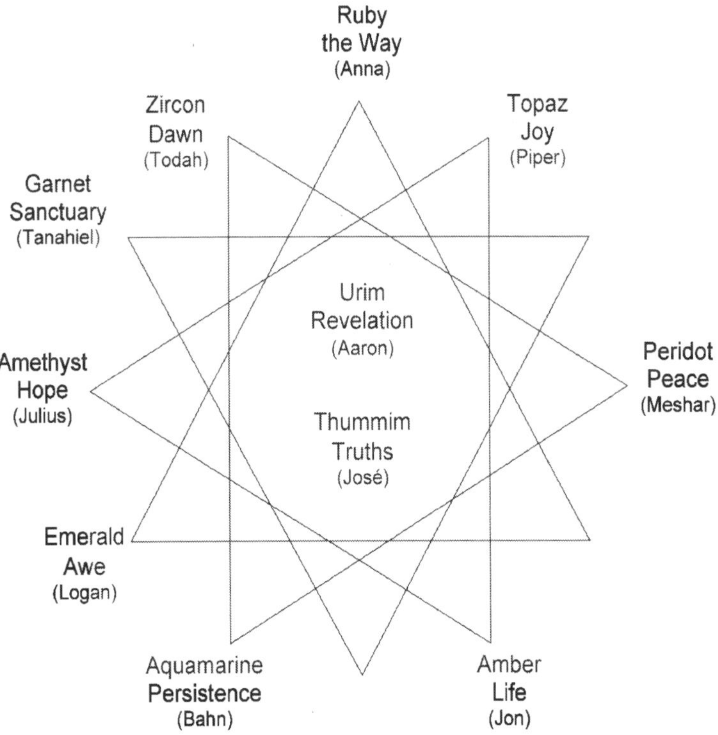

In an age where cloning had been done for years, it seemed inevitable that someone would attempt to bridge the gap between the species. Initially laws forbade it. The issue already terrified some, but some scientists thought they served a calling higher than the law. And so, the cog was born. Well, not actually born, developed. The first of his kind, the scientists designed him as a male and named him Adam. Whether he would be fertile remained an open question. They hoped he would end up with all of the best traits, qualities, and characteristics of both species, but it would be like a throw of the dice, only infinitely more complex. How would the differences mix, match, and mold into a new being? As a kitty – pup he did seem to be friendly enough, although it seemed strange to hear a dog purr. Dogs and cats share many traits: nuzzling you, licking you, sensing when you need them or want them. And with the cog the scientists seem to have been fortunate to have gotten the best from both species. One of the purely dog parts of him, though, did prevail. Although exceptionally trainable as far as obedience went, nothing could convince him to use a litter box! Play in it yes, but defecate, absolutely not! Perhaps he had figured out that if he did not use the litter box they would have to let him outside and he loved being outside. In a moment of inattention he escaped, but he had no training to survive in the wild, and it nearly killed him.

Walking through the forest on her way to her and Teedhar's favorite tree, Todah heard an interesting sound, halfway between a whimper and a yell. There, just off the path, lay the strangest looking small dog, or perhaps a cat? She eventually picked him up and carried him home. She nursed him back to health. Only part of his lab tag remained on his collar, enough to identify him as Adam the cog and the date that ended his incubation. It is said that a dog is man's best friend, but animals can perceive the spiritual as well as the emotional. Of course, they became inseparable. Adam's spiritual receptivity not only aided in his perception of Teedhar, but also helped keep Todah out of harm's way. That made Teedhar's guardianship easier. One day Adam kept sniffing and pawing at the pocket in which Todah kept the Dawn stone, so she decided to show it to him. When she opened her hand, he sniffed it, sat back on his haunches and lay down purring. Suddenly, he was up and off like a shot for the front door where he stood pawing at it and making a racket the likes of which they had never heard from cat or dog. Todah opened the door, and Adam took off like a shot again! He went straight into the forest at a dead run, still making the most unusual sound. They chased after him, Todah running and Teedhar flying, and found him at their favorite oak digging furiously. At first Todah, angered, called out, "Stop Adam, stop! You're ruining our special place!" Then Adam did stop and pointed like only a cog can at the hole he had dug.

Todah sifted through the dirt at the bottom of the hole and brought up a gem of some sort. When she had cleaned it off, she found a flawless diamond, the largest she had ever seen. She sat down, Adam sat down, even Teedhar sat down.

She placed her other hand on Adam's head, and said, "I'm sorry I yelled at you, Adam. It's beautiful. I wonder what it is?"

"Ask and you shall receive," suddenly jumped into her mind. She turned to Teedhar.

"Well?" she asked.

"Adam has discovered the stone of Discernment and it shall be his," replied Teedhar just outside the range of most people's hearing, "I wondered where the archangel had hidden it."

But both Adam and Todah nodded and said together, "Yes, and thank you!"

They went back home and Todah sewed a pouch to contain the stone of Discernment. She attached it to Adam's collar in such a way that it did not bounce around when he did, which he did most of the time.

Chapter 25 - Defiance's Quest

...The light shows nothing without casting a shadow. How can there be a glorious day, unless it is preceded by the dark of night?

from the "Proverbs of the Seer"

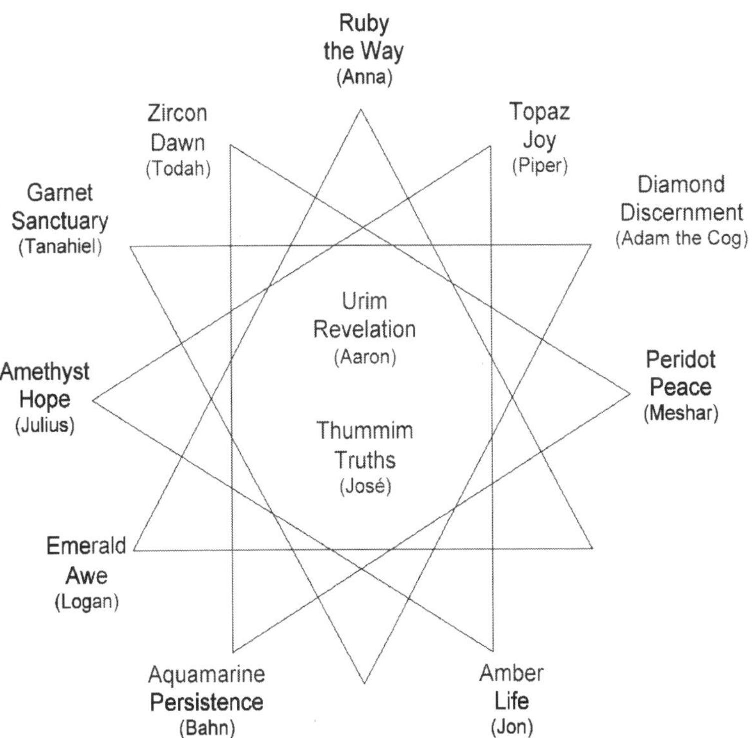

They said that it was the name that they were given for their son, "Defiance." Why would they be given that name? At least he could choose his own name later, but for now, he had no other. In their tongue "Dalatawanata" meant defiance. They called him Dal for short and true to his name he was a strong-willed child. His parents often thought that they should write a book on the art of breaking the will without breaking the spirit. He behaved well, but he held his ground to the point of obstinacy. Never rude or mean, he just knew what he wanted and was bound and determined that nothing would deter him! He would gladly give something away when he finally did get it, but try and take it away from him and prepare for a battle. Once an older bully pestered his friends. When Dal saw it, he rose to the occasion, though half the size of the bully, attacked with such ferocity that the bully was forced to flee leaving his ill-gotten gain behind. As Dal approached the day of his maturity, he began to seek in earnest how, according to their custom, he would change his name.

He went to the one tree, Chayeem, and asked, "What I should do concerning my name?"

Chayeem responded, "You will figure it out, Dal, only seek deeply within yourself to find the rest of your true essence, but thank you for asking."

Untainted by the wrong of man, Dal's connection with the Elohim remained pure and undefiled. Sometimes, however confirmation comforted the soul. So, Dal turned inside to his spirit and worshiped Elohim, basking in His presence.

Unbeknownst to Dal, by this time, all but the final stone of the twelve had been recovered. The luminescent one, the choirmaster, who had been the most wonderful and beautiful of all God's creatures before God had made man and woman, doubted the wisdom of God in making them. That doubt had led to open rebellion, his expulsion from heaven, and his darkening. As he had slithered out of the garden, the two stones, the Urim and Thummim, had been dislodged from his breastplate and lost. Other stones were also darkened and lost. Besides the stone of Revelation and Truths, that were found by Hal and Kate, there were the stones of Life and Persistence that were recovered by Jon and Bahn. Another stone had come from the seed of Chayeem, the one that Zemir had taken to the Cherubim who transformed it into the stone of Awe that Logan found in the belly of a fish. There were the stones of Heaven and Peace that Alathos took from the statue and placed in the pommels of the remnants of Hail'yk to become the two new singing swords that were given initially to Zemir and Bigtha. Bigtha's sword was later gifted to Meshar. The physically blind Anna received the Way stone, and Julius the stone of Hope, the earthquake gave Piper the Joy stone, the eagle delivered the Sanctuary stone to Tanaheil, and Teedhar's singing sword produced the Dawn stone for Todah, and Adam the cog unearthed the stone of Discernment. One final darkened stone remained to complete the stones of judgment.

The day arrived. Dal had reached his maturity, and his friends and family had gathered for the ceremony that would precede his vision quest. One by one they stepped forward to speak on his behalf.

The elder spoke reverently "His given name is Defiance, and he defies the status quo," He then dropped a token at Dal's feet.

Another stepped forward and continued, "He defies injustice."

Another spoke, "He rises to the task, seeking mercy and bringing hope."

Another spoke, "He has kept his life pure of entanglements and the inappropriate."

This continued until an embarrassingly large pile of tokens lay at his feet. Finally the elder raised his hand stopping any more from coming forward.

He then intoned, "And what shall we call you from this day forward?"

Dal looked solemnly at those around him. He felt truly and completely blessed. "I shall be called, Defiant Hawk, searing the night skies. But all of you may still call me Dal." He launched himself into the sky and began his quest for the vision of his destiny. He flew all the way to the garden's center and returned to the one tree, Chayeem.

"Welcome young hawk, called defiant by some," boomed the Tree. "I see that you are on the quest to discover your destiny,"

"Yes my Lord," the hawk answered.

The tree continued, "Do you think you will find it in a single day?"

"I would hope to at least find the beginning of its direction, sir," spoke the hawk reluctantly.

"Yes, you would," chuckled the Tree. "And I can at least aid you with that part."

"Thank you, sir," said the hawk solemnly.

The tree began again. "When the dark one slithered out of the garden, which way did he go?"

Dal looked intently eastward and frowned. "I believe he followed man to the east, taking his darkness with him."

"Yes, he did. And why did he choose that direction?" The Tree's voice seemed to reflect the hawk's frown.

"He wanted to continue in his attempt to tarnish your finest creation, especially Dawn," spoke the hawk in almost a whisper.

"You are right again! Are you sure you are only a young hawk?" The Tree laughed again.

"I've tried to listen and learn from my elders, especially the eagle." The hawk no longer whispered.

"A good choice!" said the Tree, "as he is wonderfully wise. Follow the path the dark one took and see what you will find there, but be careful and alert. It is a difficult, dark, and dangerous path."

Although the ominous words seemed to contain a note of sadness, the tone of the Tree still held hope. Dal took to the skies and headed east. He tipped his wing in greeting to the Cherubim as he passed. Once out of the garden, he found that the earth had become a desolate place. Its beauty was now tarnished and distorted. Cooperation between the plants, animals, and man corrupted into competition for resources. The path the dark one slithered as he followed after man darkened distinctively, and Dal flew along it until he came to a spot devoid of all light and life. Just as the morning sun broke over the nearby hills and flooded the valley in light, he came to that one spot, a circle about three cubits in width. Dal landed just outside the circle. Even with his sharp vision he could not penetrate the darkness he found there. He asked, seemingly to no one in particular, "Should I enter the circle?" He felt a strong impression that he should, but with extreme care. He took a tentative step into the circle and, while feeling disoriented nothing else happened. He stepped closer to the center and found an object that seemed to be sucking in all of the surrounding light and life. He felt powerfully torn between the urge to run away and an equally powerful urge to pick it up.

"Chayeem, what should I do?" He whispered. Slowly a being of anti-radiant darkness arose out of the dark circle of earth beyond the object.

"You may not have it!" It spoke with an nearly palatable menace.

Dal countered with, "I do not serve you, I serve the one tree!"

The being visibly shuddered, but laughed ominously. "I conquered and destroyed the Tree," it countered, "after you left the garden!" Suddenly the air shimmered to display a vision of the one tree burned beyond recognition, the garden a smoking ruin.

"You are a liar and the father of lies!" the hawk challenged, took a large step forward, and grasped the object. Dal did not drop dead, slain by the power of the dark stone although a coldness and darkness worse than any midnight enveloped him. Even so, he did not shirk or flee the experience. He embraced the shadow and pushed beyond it to know that in his weakness and frailty his Lord, the Tree, strengthened him with a power that rendered the dark stone's evil ineffective. He now possessed the Night stone. Some of the stones had a twin, like the Way and the Sanctuary stones, the Urim and the Thummim. Other stones balanced one another. The Night stone balanced the Dawn stone. Now all had been recovered, yet not all brought together.

PART 8

THE SANCTUARY

Chapter 26 - Discovering the Sanctuary

Why do I hide a thing?

Some things are hidden to "age"and become more flavorful, others because they are too precious to be seen by all, and still others are hidden until the time is ripe for them to be revealed.

From the "Book of Secrets"

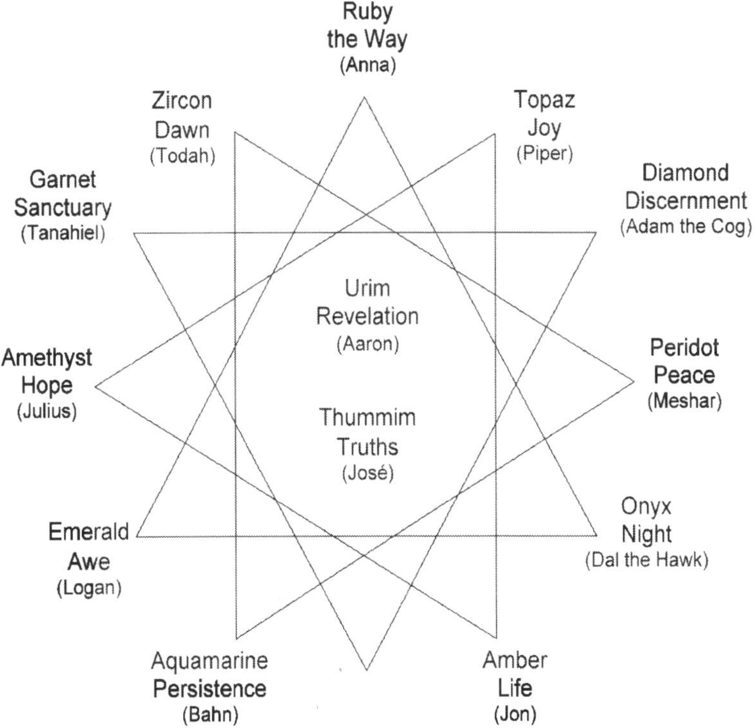

On a beautiful sunny September morning, Anna, Logan, and Tanahiel all left the farm to go on their picnic. Logan carried their lunch in his day pack, and they each had a water bottle clipped to their belt. After walking down the lane for the better part of the morning, they strode off into the forest following some kind of an animal trail. How could blind Anna walk a path like this, uncannily well in the middle of the forest, without a care in the world that she might stumble or walk into something? Anna, who always now wore the Way stone next to her heart asked, "Did you both bring your stones with you?" Tanahiel responded, "Yes, I have mine," and Logan added, "Me, too." For a while now they had been climbing into the hills. "Good," she called back to them and then, nonchalantly. "We should probably stop for lunch soon." No sooner had she said that, then they broke into a small sun-lit meadow where the hill had plateaued for the moment. Anna stopped for some reason, and Logan stepped up beside her. "This looks like a good place," gestured Logan. And sure enough, in the center of the meadow rested a large, flat stone they could use as their table, surrounded by a number of smaller flat stones upon which they could sit. "Hmm," mused Tanahiel, "this reminds me of a scene out of a fairy tale. At least, I think it was a fairy tale." "Which fairy tale?" asked Anna. "I'm not sure," responded Tanahiel, "but I think it had a happy ending." And they chuckled in harmony with one another.

Logan had obviously packed their lunch with a great deal of purpose, evident as he unpacked it. He smoothed out a small plain tablecloth on the makeshift table and then set out portions of fruit, cheese, bread, and what looked like chocolate for each of them.

"How come the chocolate has not melted?" asked Tanahiel. "We have been walking in the hot sun all this morning, at least until we entered the forest?"

"The chocolate was packed in the center of everything, away from the heat of the sun and the heat of my back," came his simple answer.

They bowed their heads and gave thanks, then ate their small meal while sharing joy and laughter. Only few crumbs remained of their meal which they brushed into the grass beside them for the animals.

Suddenly, they all looked at each other.

"Did you hear that?" questioned Anna.

"You mean the voice saying, 'It is time.'" replied Logan trembling with anticipation.

"Yes, that!"

"Let's place our stones on the table." Anna removed hers from around her neck and placed it on the table. Tanahiel removed hers from its linen pouch and placed on the table, and Logan took his from his pocket and did the same.

"Move them together," continued Anna and they did so until they touched in triangle. A large billowy cloud had covered the sun and its shadow had fallen on them. A hole opened up in the cloud and the sun shone through, one brilliant ray pointing to an exit from the meadow and back into the forest. They all pointed together, "That way," they said. They each grabbed their stone. Logan folded up the tablecloth, put it into his pack and shouldered it. Then hand in hand they left the meadow through the opening that the ray of sun indicated.

They went down the forested hill a short distance until they came to a stream. For some reason the stream seemed almost cheerful, and it broke the intensity which had come over them while following the direction the sunbeam had pointed out. They followed the stream for about a mile and turned a corner to face the mouth of a large cave.

"Well," said Logan, "we were following the path, which followed the stream, and both enter the cave. I guess we go in."

"But it will be dark in there," countered Tanahiel.

"Take out your stones and hold my hands," said Anna, who had taken her stone out to rest on top of her blouse. Tanahiel took the Sanctuary stone in her left hand and grasped Anna's with her right. Logan placed the Awe stone in his right hand and held Anna's with his left. Together the three of them entered the cave.

Though the three of them could easily walk side by side on the broad path, it soon became too dark for them to see.

Tanahiel complained, "I can't see."

And Logan added, "Me either."

"It's OK. I can see just fine," said Anna.

"Oh, that's comforting." chuckled Tanahiel, but she knew that often the Way stone gave Anna the ability to see spiritually even though she could not see physically.

"The path stays straight and level and there are no obstacles. Just hold your stones in front of you." They walked for another mile, then suddenly burst from what seemed like the exit of a tunnel. They had seen no light ahead of them. One moment they walked in great darkness and the next moment they stepped into the light. That should have been amazing enough, but in front of them stood a centaur, a large horse with the upper body of a man. He held a short bow in his right hand and quiver of arrows on his back. They froze shocked silent.

Logan got his voice back first.

He exclaimed,"Are you Sagittarius, the archer of legend?"

When the centaur laughed, all their tension and fear melted away. "No! I am Alathos, the guardian of the gateway. At least for today."

Logan continued almost brazenly. "You are only Alathos for the day or guardian for the day?"

The centaur laughed again. "I like you, little man," he said to the dwarf. "I am guardian for today. May I ask how you found this place?" The three of them simultaneously held forth their stones.

Anna said, "We obeyed the voice."

"Ah..." he boomed, "that would make sense. Welcome to the Sanctuary. And you are?"

Anna stepped forward, "I'm Anna and I'm blind. Well, most of the time, but I can see you Mr. Alathos."

"Nice to meet you, Anna."

The dwarf stepped forward, bowed perfunctorily and said, "and I am Logan." Alathos continued, "Ah yes, I should've guessed. You will like it here very much, Logan. You were made for this place."

And then Tanahiel, "and I am Tanahiel." Since Logan had bowed, she curtsied.

"Yes, Tanahiel. You have already met a great friend of mine. I believe he gave you the stone for which this place is named."

She blurted out, "You know the eagle? Is he here?"

Alathos chuckled and said, "Yes, he is here, but unfortunately I can't let you come in any further at this time. It is imperative that you go back and lead the rest of those who are called to come back with you, back to this place. And bring the Ark of God with you, too."

Tanahiel replied, "OK," and immediately turned around, as did Logan.

"When should we come back?" asked Anna.

Alathos replied, "He will let you know."

To which Anna responded, "I should have guessed that. Thank you, Alathos, it's been nice to meet you." And she turned around, too. The three of them walked back into the cave, that was no cave, retraced their steps, and returned to the farm.

Chapter 27 - Travel to the Sanctuary

And when My Ark is restored, it will be taken to its new resting place and once again it will become the center of wonder and awe.

from a "Maccabean Fragment"

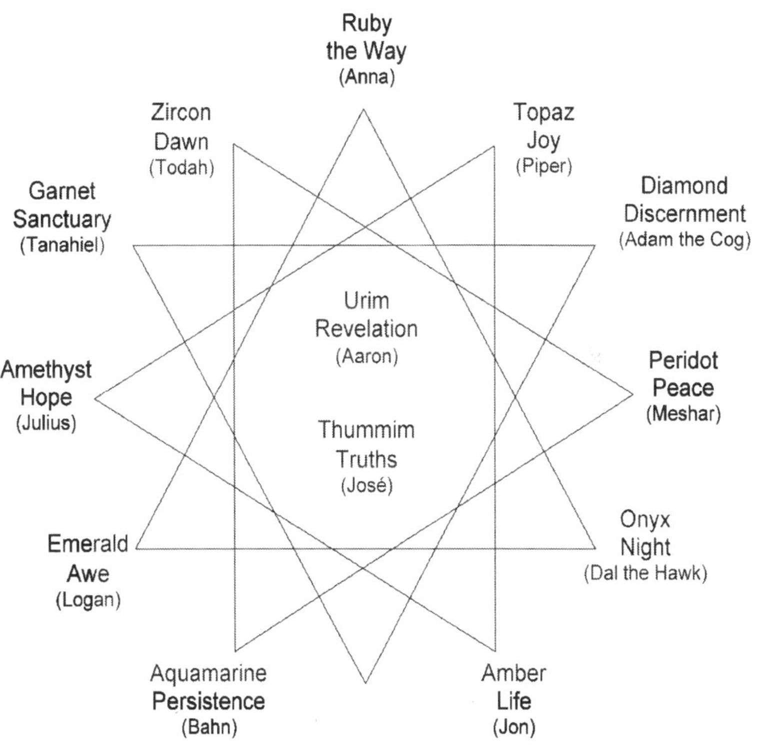

The three of them, Tanahiel, Logan, and Anna, returned to the farm at twilight, just in time for supper. They quickly washed, freshened up, and joined the others as they all sat at the table. Aaron said a wonderfully short blessing, as the entire family felt famished. Anna and Judy often sat next to each other. Both being blind, they seemed to share a second sight, especially as the food passed around the table. They anticipated each other's needs and virtually without error passed the plate into the other person's hands. Oh, they told stories of comical exceptions to this, but, even though they could not see, no one treated them as handicapped in the least. The deference shown to them displayed itself as value and honor, particularly evident with Anna, who, while in possession of the Way stone, seemed able to see spiritually. Often she could even see what others could not see, like the angels who stood with the Ark before they revealed themselves to the others.

As usual, everyone shared the events of their day in joyful conversation. Then Aaron jangled his spoon against his glass to get everyone's attention. "I would like to hear from our three adventurers. What was your day like?" As best they could, in almost a "tag-team" where they filled in the blanks for each other, they recounted their adventure. As they spoke of it, from the voice, to the sunbeam, to the cave and the centaur, they had everyone on the edge of their seat.

Jon piped up, "A centaur?"

But Aaron cut in, "Excuse me. You each have a special stone?"

Logan reached into his pocket and placed his on the table, while Tanahiel removed hers from its pouch and placed it on the table, and Anna removed hers from around her neck and did the same. Anna reluctantly released hers, but you could still see a beautiful, large ruby.

"And they each have names?" he asked.

Anna replied first, "Yes, mine is the Way stone."

"And mine, the Awe stone," continued Logan.

"And mine the Sanctuary stone," completed Tanahiel.

At the word Sanctuary, Aaron nearly collapsed like he did when he first touched the Urim.

"This is remarkable," said Aaron. "And José and I have the Urim and the Thummim of old!" They both placed their stones on the table. Jon retook control of the conversation,

"I have the Life stone." And he placed it on the table.

Bahn said, "and I the stone of Persistence," as his stone joined the others on the table.

Piper spoke up, "I have the Joy stone," and she placed it on the table.

Finally there was Julius, "and I the stone of Hope." He placed the final stone on the table.

"This is utterly amazing," said Aaron. "The eight of us each has a special stone. What could be the meaning of this?"

Anna spoke, "and when we put our three stones together we were shown which direction to leave out of the meadow by the sunbeam. It was the direction that eventually led us to the cave, which was more like a tunnel." She moved her stone to where she sensed Logan's lay while Tanahiel did the same on his other side. As they touched, it was as though the air in the room trembled, shimmering slightly.

Anna spoke again. "The angel Ayah is standing behind you, Aaron, and Anan is behind you, José."

The angels asked in chorus, "And at the Sanctuary, you met…?"

"We met the centaur, Alathos. He told us that we couldn't go any further into the sanctuary until we came back here and returned with all of those who were called to come. Oh, and we were to bring the Ark of God with us."

Aaron then spoke out, "God, who are those called to come?" One by one they all stood, each of those who had a stone. Even Judy and Mary who did not have stones stood. Aaron spoke again, "And when should we go?"

The angels answered, "Tomorrow!"

That next morning after cleaning up from breakfast, they all met around the dining room table for prayer and worship. When they finished and Jon stood.

He asked, "Anna, are the angels here?"

"Yes, Jon," she responded.

Jon then prayed, "Lord, what should we take with us?"

Aaron then stood, "We won't need much; a light lunch, a change of clothes, our personal bedding and toiletries."

Jon continued, "Then let's gather what we need and meet in the basement in say, an hour?" Heads nodded all around and each departed to gather their belongings. As everyone left, Jon leaned over to Aaron,

He whispered, "Do you have any idea how we are going to get the Ark out of its resting place?"

Aaron whispered back, "Not a clue."

The entire entourage assembled in the basement with their bundled belongings, quite a sight. Some looked ready to go on a hiking trip, complete with backpacks and walking sticks. Others looked only prepared for a short stroll in the park with a picnic lunch. Gathered in a semi-circle, kneeling on the basement floor,

Aaron led them in prayer. "God, you have called us to take Your Ark to the Sanctuary. We are trusting you to lead us, guide us, and protect us. How shall we proceed?"

Back returned a nearly audible voice ringing in each of their minds and hearts, "A little child will lead you. In this case three whose hearts are still child-like: Logan, Anna, and Tanahiel. They will be followed by Aaron and José, My Ark carried by My two angels, followed by Jon and Mary, Judy and Todd, with Julius and Piper acting as the rear guard."

Aaron leaned over to Jon and whispered, "Did you hear that?" Jon nodded. Aaron continued still whispering, "Well, that at least solves the question of how we will transport the Ark, but how are we going to get it out of the cavern?"

Jon whispered again, "I'm sure He must have something figured out. Let's just go with it."

Aaron spoke out louder, "How many of you just heard God speak to you in answer to our prayer?" They all raised a hand and awe enveloped them all. Jon stood first, stepped to the blanket that covered the entrance and pulled it back.

The rest of them stood, and they all assembled in the order God had just spoken, leaving a space for Ayah and Anan. When they had done that, the two angels appeared in their places and they all entered into the cave and then the cavern. Logan, Anna, and Tanahiel moved around the Ark and positioned themselves on the far side facing the stone wall. Anna removed the Way stone from her blouse to hang outside of her jacket. Tanahiel and Logan now each had a stone in one hand and joined their other hand to Anna's. The two angels bent and picked up the Ark, covered in its veil, by its poles. Without a sound, or the opening of a portal, or anything at all, the three young people proceeded to walk straight through the stone wall like it didn't exist. The angels followed them with the Ark, and each of the pairs turned to smile at one another as they did the same. Bringing up the rear, Julius and Piper followed those before them. Shaking their heads in astonishment they walked right through the stone wall.

Outside, they proceeded to follow the route the three had previously taken to the meadow. As they crested one hill, Anan spoke, "We need to stop for a moment. They did, and he and Ayah set down the Ark. Suddenly, they all heard, from ahead of them, a fast approaching and low flying airship. Anan raised his hands and a billowy cloud covered them from the sight of the ship. It whizzed past them all heading back in the direction of the farm. As one they all turned around. They heard the sound of a huge explosion and, even at that distance, could feel the concussion as the farm was destroyed. Smoke and flames rose high in the cloudy mid-morning sky.

"No turning back now," muttered Julius.

Jon added, "The Triparteum has destroyed us! Well, they probably think they have!" The rest of the group stood speechless at their deliverance from destruction.

Anan spoke again, "We may continue." The two of them bent to pick up the Ark, as the rest of them turned to resume their journey. The cloud that had covered them, now followed them, staying just above them, protecting them from any aerial view. They continued to the meadow where they stopped for their light lunch. They gathered in a small circle, except for the angels who stood at each end of the Ark, offered thanks, and shared their meal.

The rest of their journey proceeded uneventfully. Having passed this way before, the three did not even need a sunbeam to show them the way out of the meadow, but they continued to hold hands and their gems as they led the parade to the tunnel. They mostly traveled in silence, still wrapped in the awe of the morning: the astonishment of walking through a stone wall, the destruction of the farm after they had left, and the cloud that overshadowed them. As they entered the tunnel and it began to be too dark for them to see, the angels lifted the Ark's poles to their shoulders, freeing their arms. With one hand steadying the pole on their shoulder, they drew their flaming swords with the other. Now everyone had plenty of light for them to continue, although Anna did not need any light. In this manner they continued until they walked into the daylight of the other side. There, of course, they met Alathos the Centaur, who stood almost as tall as the angels. He knelt on one knee, "Greetings in the name of He who was, and is, and is to come. Welcome to His Sanctuary." When he knelt, they realized that two angels stood behind him. Did they always come in twos?

A presence or something, about Ayah and Anan tended to inspire a strong combination of awe and terror. Perhaps referred to as "the fear of the Lord." These two angels who now stepped forward gave a quite different impression. Decidedly friendly, these angels smiled a lot, where Ayah and Anan's expressions tended towards stern.

"Good afternoon," the one said, "I am Zemir." He almost sang the words. "If Ayah and Anan would please follow me with the Ark, Alathos will escort the rest of you to the village." The company split into those two groups, the two angels with the Ark following Zemir.

The other angel stepped around Alathos who still knelt. Alathos asked, "Anna, would you like to ride with me to the village?"

"I most certainly would, sir!" she replied, walked over to him, and the other angel hoisted her onto Alathos' back.

The other angel whispered to Anna. "I am Zek. Although you have not known it, I have been with you your entire life. It is a joy that you finally are allowed to see me." Large tears welled up in Anna's blind eyes and spilled out onto her blouse as she realized the truth of what he said.

She questioned, "But since I found the Way stone I have seen the other angels, why not you?"

He softly replied, "I don't know. You will have to ask Him sometime."

Alathos stood and announced, "Then off to village we go!" to which Logan sang in typical dwarfish fashion, "Hi ho, hi ho, it's off to the village we go…" and the rest of the parade followed them as Alathos led them through the forest.

Along their trek, Anna asked Alathos, "From the outside world it seemed we entered a cave, but when we exited it on this side it seemed like we had been in a tunnel. Can you explain this?"

"I can," replied Alathos. "You did enter a cave, one that you are still in. The Sanctuary is a large underground cavern that contains all that you can see and much more."

"We are still underground?" she exclaimed, "It doesn't feel like it."

"When I was asked to leave Eden by Chayeem I was asked to establish this place. It is a special place, a protected place, designed for what is coming. The time ahead has many names, the Great

Tribulation, the Day of Wrath, Time of Judgement. Regardless of the name, it will be a time of great difficulties, and this place was built to take you and many like you through these times."

"But if this is all underground, why does it seem like daylight here?" she questioned.

Alathos continued, "As you recall, in the beginning, God spoke and created light. He has many sources of light, more than you can imagine, and some of those He uses to enlighten this place as though it were day."

"But the ceiling of this cave looks like it is just a cloudy sky," she said still in awe.

"Ah yes, the firmament," he chuckled, "you will find there is no rain here, but each night a dew will water the ground."

"There will be both day and night here in the cave?" she bemused.

"Yup, its as simple as that," he chuckled as they emerged from the forest.

The village appeared unlike anything they had expected or could have imagined. They passed what seemed to function as a cooking building and an outdoor dining facility, and found a vast circle of identical cottages, all without doors. Who would need doors in God's Sanctuary? It would have taken a person quite a while to walk around the circle and count them all.

Alathos shared, "I will give you about an hour to get settled and then we will meet in the dining area for supper." He assigned them their cottages in almost the same "two by two" order in which they had traveled with a few exceptions. Anna, Tanahiel, and Piper took the first one. As they moved to the right, Aaron and José settled in the next, then Jon and Mary, Judy and Todd. Julius and Logan moved into the final one. As the cottages continued to the right, you could see another cooking and dining facility about six hundred cubits away. The cottages measured about twenty cubits square and contained a bedroom with two or three single beds. These could be pushed together for a couple. Each occupant had a small dresser and all shared a common bathroom that seemed to be gravity fed, with water drawn from the well near the cooking building, and a sitting room filled with some sparse wooden furniture. They spent the next hour settling in and personalizing their living spaces, and then all met at the dining facility with about twenty of their neighbors.

Logan had found heaven; animals showed up everywhere. He found this out by talking to the dog that lived next door. The dog did NOT live with his owner. He lived with his friend, who just happened to be human. The dog was not a pet, he was an equal, plus all the animals in the sanctuary spoke to each other, to the humans, and to the angels. Logan had assumed that he could understand the dog based on his gift and possession of the Awe stone. Caleb, the dog next door, told him, "Nope, everybody understands everybody else." Caleb then swore him to secrecy, saying, "You will find out why tonight at supper."

Zemir knelt before the Tree, the son of Chayeem, in his human form. The Tree didn't require him to be in his human form, but because the Tree was only as tall as a man, it seemed more reverent not to be a ten foot tall angel in his presence.

"You called my Lord," Zemir sang.

"Yes, Zemir, thanks for coming," sang the Tree also and chuckled. He might as well sing along with Zemir. "I am sure you recall when Alathos made the two singing swords from the remains of Hail'yk and entrusted Hashamayeem to you and Meshar to Bigtha."

"I do, my Lord," responded Zemir a bit puzzled.

"And Gomed was given the Meshar and taught the dance of the two swords by the old man," the Tree continued to sing, he was enjoying this.

"Yes?" questioned Zemir.

"By the way, did Gomed ever realize that you were the old man?" asked the Tree.

"No Sir, I don't believe he did," replied Zemir.

"Well, Gomed finally mastered the singing sword Meshar, as I knew he would, and I changed his name to Meshar, and had him unscrew the end of the sword Meshar's and gave him the stone Meshar, the stone of Peace. Wow, that is quite a sentence. You should try to say that quickly three times," he chuckled again.

Zemir frowned. "You want me to repeat what you just said three times quickly?"

"No, no," still chuckling, "I was just making an observation. However, you may remove your sword from its sheath for me." Zemir complied. "Now, unscrew the end of its hilt and drop its stone into your hand." Zemir did that too. When the sapphire, Hashamayeem, from the sword Hashamayeem, fell into his hand, he nearly collapsed from the beauty that overwhelmed him.

"There," said the Tree, "you are now the proud possessor of the stone of Heaven!" The very air seemed to reverberate as he spoke.

"Thanks you, Sir!" Zemir stammered barely able to speak, let alone get up off his knees.

"We will soon have need of all of the stones," began the Tree again, "and I wanted you to be prepared. You are dismissed." Zemir got shakily to his feet and turned to go.

"Oh, Zemir," intoned the Tree. Zemir turned back around. "You need to know, I am especially fond of you." Zemir smiled, turned again, away from the Tree, and continued to smile all the way back to supper.

Chapter 28 - Life & Love in the Sanctuary

And I am preparing a place. It will be a safe place, a resting place, a place of awe and wonder, a place of preparation, a sacred place. I am preparing My Sanctuary.

from the "Seer's Vision"

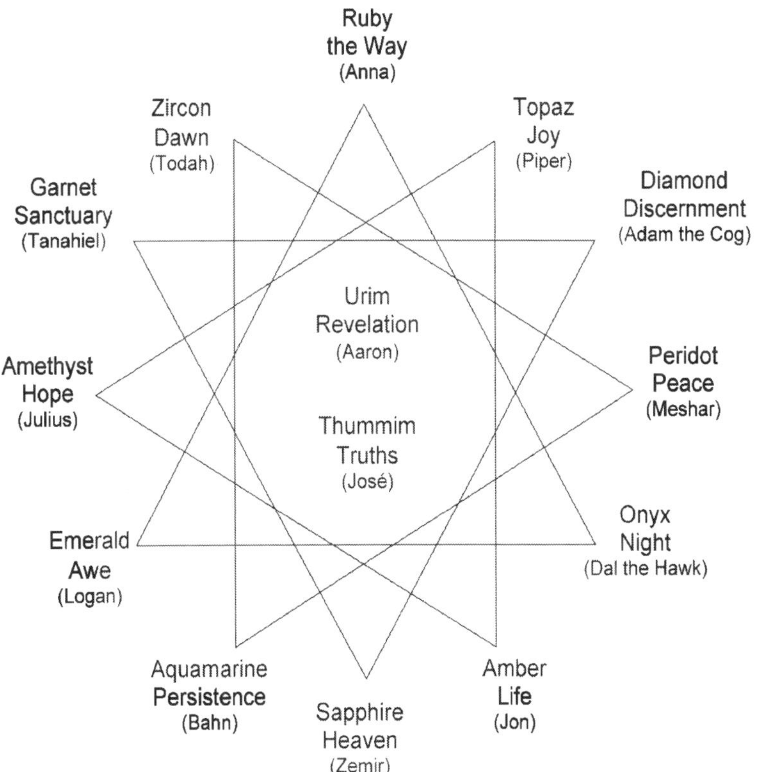

They found supper served buffet style. Two tables set arranged with all kinds of raw fruits, vegetables, and nuts. Two more tables stood piled with cooked vegetables, wild rice, and beverages. They noticed there was a conspicuous absence of meat. Welcome back to the Garden of Eden, but what a feast. Their new neighbors, not all of whom were human, joined them. The angel Zimri came, but in his human form. He no longer stood ten feet tall and he had no wings, but they recognized him. A number of animals and birds came to eat, including a large hawk who introduced himself as Dal. Alathos, the centaur, stood up and acted as Master of Ceremonies after he had led the group in thanksgiving for the Lord's provision. "You will find the Sanctuary to be a wonderful place, but it is not simply a vacation stop. We each have jobs to perform, and you will have the opportunity to choose how you will serve the community." He then introduced a young woman named Todah. "Todah is one of our worship leaders. We believe that worship is a lifestyle, but it still requires leadership. If you would like to find out more concerning that opportunity, chat with her." Todah stood near another angel named Ted (short for Teedhar) who seemed particularly attached to her. "I would also like to introduce you to Meshar." An extremely fit man stood up. "He is in charge of our militia, but you will find it quite different than its name suggests," he continued. "Bigtha is our head gardener, which is separate from the crop farming function," he said, addressing that remark to Jon. "Then there is cooking and all the tasks associated with that, and working with our variety of domesticated animals." He smiled his infectious smile at Logan. "I work in wood and metal, and there is a myriad of other opportunities. Come see me and we will get you placed somewhere for tomorrow morning." He stopped and took a deep breath. "There is one more thing." A number of their new neighbors got up from their tables and headed into the cooking facility as Todah broke out in the most amazingly beautiful worship song. Each of their new neighbors returned with a bowl of cut up fruit which, as the song ended, they raised to the heavens. Alathos spoke again, "This is the fruit of the Tree of Life. Chayeem is His name. You have not met Him yet, but His Son lives in our midst, and since the dawn of time we have had the joyful privilege of partaking of His fruit. Please join us in eating a piece. In the Name of He who was, who is, and who will ever be!" Alathos ate a piece of the fruit as did everyone there, human, angel, bird, animal, even those who seemed mythical like Alathos. They felt filled with renewed life, still the surprises continued. The hawk Dal took wing to land on Alathos' back and proclaimed, "Now it will be rather apparent why there was no meat on the buffet table. We don't eat each other." A deep chuckle rippled through the gathering. He continued, "It is with great joy that I bring an end to this meal and welcome you into our fellowship." Wow, the hawk could talk. Each of the newcomers looked at one another in astonishment as they realized the truth of this. The Life provided by Chayeem's fruit gave them all the ability to understand one another. Having been dismissed, they gathered their dishes and bussed them back to the cooking facility where the dishwashing team gladly received them.

As they made their way back towards their cottages, Julius meandered over to Judy and Todd and said a bit sheepishly. "Judy, I was wondering if you would like to go for a walk with me?" Todd had been holding her hand as he guided her back to their quarters. They both smiled at him and Todd turned with her to face him.

"Thank you, Julius," she replied, "I would like that." Although blind, her hearing had become exceptionally acute, and she had easily recognized his voice. Todd offered her hand to Julius, who took it in his, his sheepishness extending into a smile. Todd continued to their cottage while Julius and Judy walked between two of the cottages and into the orchard and garden that seemed to make up a large portion of the area in the middle of the large circle of cottages.

"We are walking through the most wonderfully immaculate orchard and garden I have ever seen. The path we are on is flat and without obstacles," he shared, "so you need not worry about stumbling." As they exited the garden they found a statue of indeterminate age, marred by the passage of time, surrounded by a small spring fed pool. Behind it stood a pavilion. Julius continued describing these things to Judy as they walked further. He stopped at the pavilion's steps, helped her up them, opened the screen door and led her in. "It is much larger in here than it looked on the outside," he said. "In the middle of this pavilion is a small circular stone wall, about a cubit tall. Behind the wall is another smaller garden of herbs and a single tree, about the height of a man. Lets sit here on the wall for a moment." He guided her to sit on the short stone wall and there they sat. He continued holding her hand.

Julius said, "I was going to show you a magic trick, but I would have to explain it all to you and it wouldn't be nearly as magical."

She laughed. "That's OK, it's the thought that counts."

He went on, "I could tell you a joke." She nodded as he continued, "A homeless man was walking along the beach when he found a bottle. He thought that he might be able to sell it and make some money. So, he picked it up and started cleaning it up, rubbing it with his sleeve. All of a sudden a genie popped out and said, 'I will grant you three wishes, but only three wishes, so wish carefully.' So the homeless man said, 'I would love to be married to a beautiful, loving woman!' POOF!! And he is! 'For my second wish, I would love to be rich.' POOF!! He suddenly looks very wealthy, dressed in designer clothes, and standing next to a nice car. 'Okay,' says the genie, 'what is your third and final wish? 'Hmm,' said the homeless man, 'this is something I have always wanted. I never want to have to work another day in my life!' 'Okay.' says the genie. POOF!! He is turned back into the single homeless man again!" Judy's snicker turned into a full fledged belly laugh, wonderful to hear.

Then she added, "Julius, that was sad."

He replied, "There is a sequel." Before she could stop him, he continued, "When Jack heard about the homeless man's luck at the beach, he went out there with his metal detector. After about an hour of searching, he heard the sound he'd been waiting for: 'Beep, beep, beep.' He knelt down and dug up an old, absolutely decrepit looking lantern. He brushed the sand off it, but nothing happened. He took his handkerchief out of his back pocket and started polishing it. Finally, poof, this old decrepit genie pops out and in a gruff, raspy voice says, 'You can have one wish and you can not wish for any more wishes!' Jack responded, 'But the homeless man got three wishes!' 'Look!' said the Genie, 'Do you want your wish or not?' 'OK, ok,' said Jack, 'Look, I'm afraid of flying and get really sea sick, but I have always wanted to go to Hawaii. I would like a bridge constructed from the mainland to Hawaii.' 'What?' shrieked the genie, 'Do you have any idea what that will cost to build and the maintenance it will take to keep it up? Have you got anything else?' 'Oh,' said Jack, 'Well, I have always wanted to understand why women think the way they do?' The Genie responded, 'Do you want two lanes or four?'" Judy burst out laughing again, grasped his arm and snuggled close.

"That was funny," she said, "but it was not so funny too. Why do women think the way they do?"

Then she realized she heard someone else laughing. They both looked around. There was no one there.

Then the Tree behind them spoke. "It's OK, it's just me. You are quite a humorist, Julius, I really appreciate that about you." Astonished, they were both still looking for someone in the direction of the Tree.

"Who's there?" Julius ventured.

The tree responded, "Let me introduce myself. I am the son of Chayeem. I was brought to this garden a very long time ago. It is so very good to finally meet the two of you in person. How do you like your first evening in my Sanctuary?" They still could not believe that they spoke with a tree.

"You're a tree?" asked Julius.

"Well, not just any tree, but yes." he answered.

"Your…Sanctuary seems nice enough, but actually I was wondering why we are here, besides the fact that we were delivered from the Triparteum who destroyed the farm?" said Julius.

The son of Chayeem responded, "Hmmm, that's a huge question. To begin with, you brought the stones here. Oh, Judy, you weren't given a stone to bring here, but I have something else for you. I'll get to that in a minute. The other reason is that I need to prepare you."

"For what?" Julius asked more impertinently than he had intended.

"I'm afraid you will have to wait a bit for the answer to that, also. Hmmm, sometimes I seem to create more questions than I answer," the Tree chuckled.

Judy finally spoke up, "Is there anything else that You can tell us?"

"Yes!" spoke the Tree. "You will find joy here beyond what you thought was possible." Julius looked at Judy as a smile began to widen across his face. He hoped that he guessed correctly what the Tree seemed to suggest.

The tree continued speaking, "Julius, do you remember the story of Jesus, the Liberator, healing the blind man by spitting on the ground, making mud of the spittle, putting it in the man's eyes, and telling him to go wash his eyes in the pool?"

"Yes," Julius was afraid to believe what he hoped would come next.

"Would you please do that for Judy, and then take her back to the pool you passed on your way here and wash the mud out of her eyes?" Hesitantly, he complied, spitting on the ground, making mud, and putting it in her eyes. He then helped her up. They walked back to the pool, and she washed the mud from her eyes. She dried her eyes on the hem of her skirt and opened them to realize she could see again. She embraced Julius, laughing and crying all at the same time, and then hand in hand they ran back to the Tree. They fell to their knees at the foot of the Tree and, as words gushing forth like an unstopped spring, expressed their thanks.

The joy continued to multiply as they went from cottage to cottage with the good news. When Anna, Piper, and Tanahiel sat once again alone in their own cottage,

Tanahiel asked Anna, "Do you think that we should go to the Tree and see if He would like to heal your eyes?"

She smiled and replied, "No, thank you. I see more than most of you, most of the time. I am more than content just the way that I am, but thanks for asking." That night everyone slept better than they ever had before in this place of palpable peace and security.

All were up early the next morning feeling more rested than they could remember and, after a wonderful breakfast that besides the fruit, grains, and nuts of last night, also included cheese, fresh eggs, and raw milk, went off to their assignments. Mary and Judy stayed to help with cleanup and became a part of the cooking corps. Piper left to join Todah on the worship team. Logan disappeared to be with the animals. Tanahiel divided her time between Logan and the animals and Piper with the worship team. Jon joined the farming community. Julius joined the militia. The Tree called Aaron and José to a series of frequent meetings, and Alathos asked Anna to go with him back into the forest where her spiritual sight proved an unquestioned asset. Their days expanded into weeks and months of wonderful food, fellowship, service to one another, and a general awe of their surroundings. So much they hadn't expected, imagined, or even dreamed, they found at the Sanctuary. The blossoming relationship between Julius and Judy proved one of those delights. It felt almost anticlimactic that one evening after supper when they stood and Julius announced, "I would like to inform you all that Judy has agreed to become my wife!" That inspired even more joy and the planning for the first wedding the troupe had experienced in the Sanctuary.

News of their betrothal traveled like wildfire throughout the Sanctuary. Aaron and José agreed to jointly lead the ceremony, and they invited all their new friends. "Don't think you'll get a year off from the militia just because you're getting married," Meshar kidded. When the time came, Alathos led the entire company and all their friends through the forest to a part of the Sanctuary that probably no one else even knew existed. They hauled an entire banquet with them for after the ceremony. Alathos ushered them into a meadow that faced a large pool, back dropped by a beautiful small waterfall. Judy dressed modestly in white. Where she had found the material for the dress she kept a secret. She had a laurel crown of flowers in her hair. Julius, freshly shaved, was dressed plainly in his not-everyday-work clothes. After making promises to one another and sharing vows, Alathos surprised them with simple gold wedding bands that he had made at his forge. Finally, José announced to Julius that he could kiss his bride. A roar of applause, shouts, and even a few whistles greeted their first kiss. Then came songs and dances galore until Alathos announced that the time had come for the newlyweds to depart. They both climbed on his back and he galloped off to another secret place, a small cabin with a pool of its own and enough food and supplies to last the few days they would have alone until he returned for them. That night, under the familiar canopy of clouds that filled the Sanctuary's sky, they conceived a child, Hashadiel.

Chapter 29 - And God Showed Up

And once again My Pillar of Fire will be in their midst, a source of light, a symbol of protection, My very presence. "And how shall this be?" you may ask. You will re-establish the place where the anointed cherub walked.

from the "Hidden Scroll"

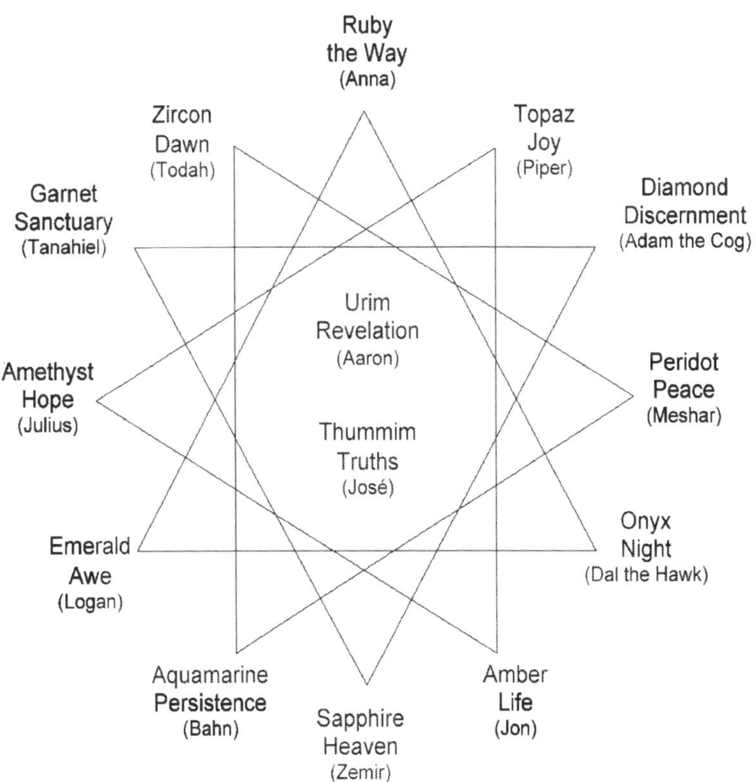

Hung around the neck of the prophet was the Urim. Hung around the neck of the priest was the Thummim. The two of them were encircled by the following; Logan, Piper, Jon, and Bahn, Zemir, Dal, Tanahiel, and Todah, Julius, Anna, Adam, and Meshar. The prophet held his staff aloft and spoke with a voice as clear as crystal. "Take off your shoes. This ground is about to become exceedingly holy and I want you to feel the full impact of it." Those who could complied. He continued, "Take out the stone that each of you possesses and hold it forth." Each of the twelve removed their stone from its resting place and held it out before them. "It is now the privilege of each of you, as individuals, to choose to relinquish your stone." One by one they knelt. as they could, at the small receptacle before them and placed their stone on it. Alathos had, at some recent point, crafted receptacles for each of the stones at his forge. Without command or coercion they all reached out and joined hands, paws, or wings with one another. The prophet began a song in a language none of them knew and yet all of them understood. By the time he got to the chorus they found that they too could sing it, and they all joined in harmonizing with one another. It seemed right and appropriate for them to do so and, as they did, the stones themselves joined in. They began sending forth their unique and individual light, and then producing an individual tone that perfectly harmonized with every other stone. Then the miracle occurred. It was not an explosion, but it might as well have been, as a pillar of fire ignited in their midst. It engulfed from the stones inward seemingly consuming the prophet, priest, and the ark. The twelve broke their ring and instantly stepped back a number of steps. This was no illusion. It was truly a pillar of fire. They felt the intense heat and heard its thunderous blazing roar. Here burned something more real than reality itself.

They stood there transfixed as it started to dawn on them. Aaron and José must have been consumed by the pillar. What about the Ark? Had it melted into a molten lump of gold and ashes? Their minds still struggled to comprehend the pillar when the Aaron stepped out of it. He seemed perfectly fine, actually smiling. He walked over to Jon and extended a hand. As he spoke, his voice still sounded like that of the Tree, "He's asking you come inside with me," he said, as he pointed back over his shoulder toward the pillar. Jon was now faced with one of the most difficult decisions of his life. How much did he trust that Aaron truly spoke for God and fully represented His thoughts, desires, and wishes? He had presented a request after all, not a demand.

God had brought them to this place. It made no sense to believe He did so just to kill them. So, he gritted his teeth and walked purposefully towards the flames. Just before the heat became unbearable, he entered the fire, and everything changed. Peace, power, and presence beyond description enveloped him. The flames had only been about a cubit thick as he walked inside of the pillar, and then everything seemed relatively the same as before. There stood Aaron, José, the Ark, the Tree, and the palpable presence of God Himself. God, the Tree, and the Prophet spoke in unison, although only the Prophet's lips moved, since only he had lips to move. "Welcome to My most holy place, Jonathan. You may come as often as you like. You do not need to be here to speak to Me nor I to you, but this is a special place and a unique experience. I know that you feel that on multiple levels. Tomorrow I would like you to begin designing exploits back into the world system, calling people to turn from their wicked ways and accept My Way. If they do so, they will be allowed to return with you to this Sanctuary. The pathway to it will continue to be obscured by illusion and power, but they will be led back here by whomever you send out. Thank you for your love, trust, and joyful obedience." They quit speaking.

Jon responded, "How will these exploits be planned, and who will go on them?"

They began again, "I will share with those whom I call together for each exploit the nature and extent of their mission. They, too, will have to trust me like you do, but all will be well with them as they follow My directions. I will send my Spirit and my Angel with them, to guide and protect them."

PART 9

THE APOCALYPSE

Chapter 30 - Adonis and His Prophet

And out of the sea of humanity one shall arise to lead the peoples, he who was dead and yet lives again. He will have no equal.

All will tremble at his coming and worship at his feet.

from the "Chronicles of the Apocalypse"

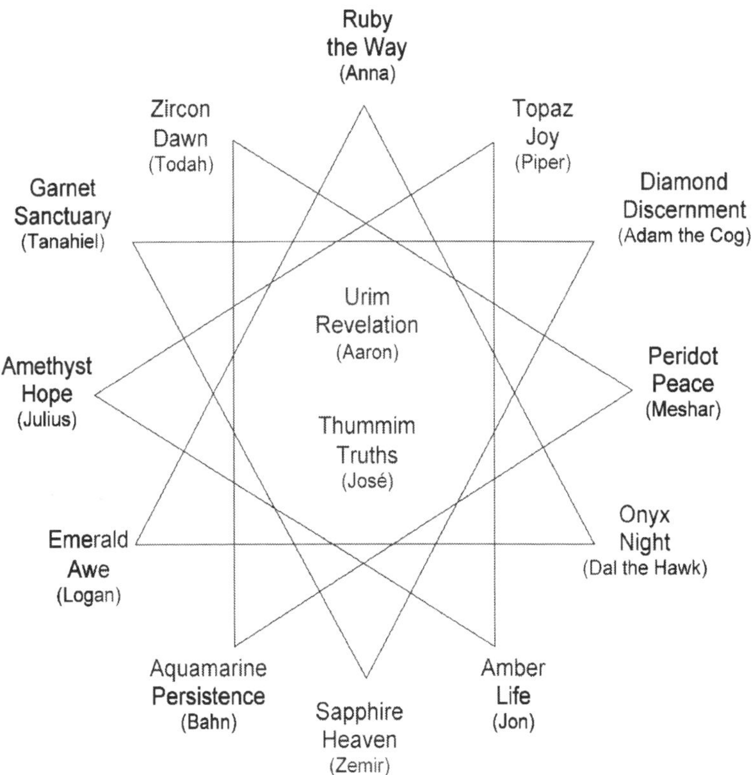

Adonis, the Chancellor, ruled totally and without question. He had through the Triparteum forged a one world government and through the Tri-World Church he had created a single unified religion, although he preferred not to call it such. Personally he worshipped "Nothing," the supreme Forces of the universe located in the unseen realms of darkness. With all of science and technology available to him, he wielded more power than any mortal man had ever before held in his own two hands. Now began the dawn of a new age, and every one heralded him as the savior of the world. He legislated a legal requirement that each individual submit to the implantation of the Quicksilver bio-microchip. He did it for the good of all mankind. The chip allowed everyone to be tracked everywhere, for their safety. The chip secured each person's personal finances and could be used at any location with a simple flick of the wrist.

The crack down on the resistors to the chip and dissidents to the Tri-World Church intensified. Initially acceptance of the chip provided extra convenience. Resistors missed out on the convenience and paid additional taxes. Then resistors to the chip could no longer buy or sell at all. Some who grew their own food and lived outside the metropolitan area could still survive. Now, however, all resistors were being hunted down. When caught they either accepted the chip or died. They treated dissidents similarly. At first they could register their assembly as a dissident group, without reprisals. Then they had to pay additional taxes, but now the Tri-World Church hunted them down and gave them the simple choice to convert to the Tri-World Church or die. They slaughtered untold hundreds and thousands every day.

At this point, the international assembly of the Tri-World Church brought Adonis before them and proclaimed him potentate. They gave him the hyphenated name -ChiyaRa, that had reportedly been provided supernaturally through one of the church's prophetic channelers, and announced that supplications and prayers could be made in his name. He became almost a deity. Media channels reported that miracles occurred at his touch and command. Adonis Ashereem-ChiyaRa had become the supreme being on the planet, and people began to worship him.

The seemingly humble way in which he lived endeared Adonis to the general public. As the wealthiest, most powerful man on the planet, he lived in a rather small old two story house in the middle of an unimpressive part of Europe. All of the latest technology filled the interior, but no one could tell that from the outside or from the immaculate gardens that surrounded the place. Adonis often televised to the world the image of this humble servant of the people working alongside his staff in the garden. Adonis understood appearances and played his role in front of the cameras like a perfectionist. The best lies are easiest to keep when they are closest to the truth. His near monk-like existence served him well and endeared him to the public

Unbeknownst to most of the world, his house sat over a huge underground bunker. Besides his swimming pool, exercise facilities, and gymnasium, this bunker contained extensive facilities used to research into the paranormal and psychic sciences. Only, Baalel, his personal prophet and medium, knew of his meditation center where he made frequent contact with the spirit world. At this deepest and darkest center of his world he now sat entranced with Baalel.

Baalel spoke, "My lord, he desires to speak to you."

Adonis responded, "Who, the Lord of Darkness?"

"No, my lord," said Baalel, "It is the Luminescent One, the source of our wisdom, power, and truth."

"What must I do?" requested Adonis.

"He requires a token of your devotion, my lord," continued Baalel.

"And what would that be?" questioned Adonis. A stone altar stood between them.

"Place yourself on the altar." Only Baalel could speak to him like this. He removed his robe and lay naked on the altar. Adonis had never seen or experienced psychic surgery before, but he had come across it in his studies. Nothing prepared him for the pain, but what would be a sacrifice if it did not involve pain? As Baalel reached into his abdomen, it seemed as though a burning blade did so, searing body, soul, and spirit. Baalel removed his bleeding kidney, although no blood spilled from the wound. He placed the kidney in a bowl next to the altar. The pain lingered, but soon began to diminish. Before the pain completely departed Adonis weakly sat up on the altar. He turned toward Baalel as the prophet reached out with the staff held in his other hand. The kidney burst into flame which consumed it immediately. A bone chilling cold accompanied the voice that overpowered even the stench of the burning flesh,

"You have done well, my servant. I am proud of you, but the battle that we wage against our adversary requires the aid of another. I want you to commission the creation of a being in your own image. Dr. Gideon Anakim will assist you. Spare no expense to bring him into being." As quickly as the flame of a snuffed candle, the voice was gone, along with the cold and the stench. Baalel placed Adonis' robe about his shoulders and helped him haltingly to his feet. "I must recover from this ordeal and prepare myself," Adonis whispered. "Make the arrangements required for me to meet Dr. Anakim at his laboratories." Baalel bowed and follow Adonis out of the chamber, a smile slowly and slyly crossing his countenance.

Chapter 31 - Made in His Image

And he will make for himself an image in his own likeness, and enliven it with the technology of his hand. It will be empowered to conduct warfare against the child of the virgin, and it will be extremely efficient in doing so.

from the "Chronicles of the Apocalypse"

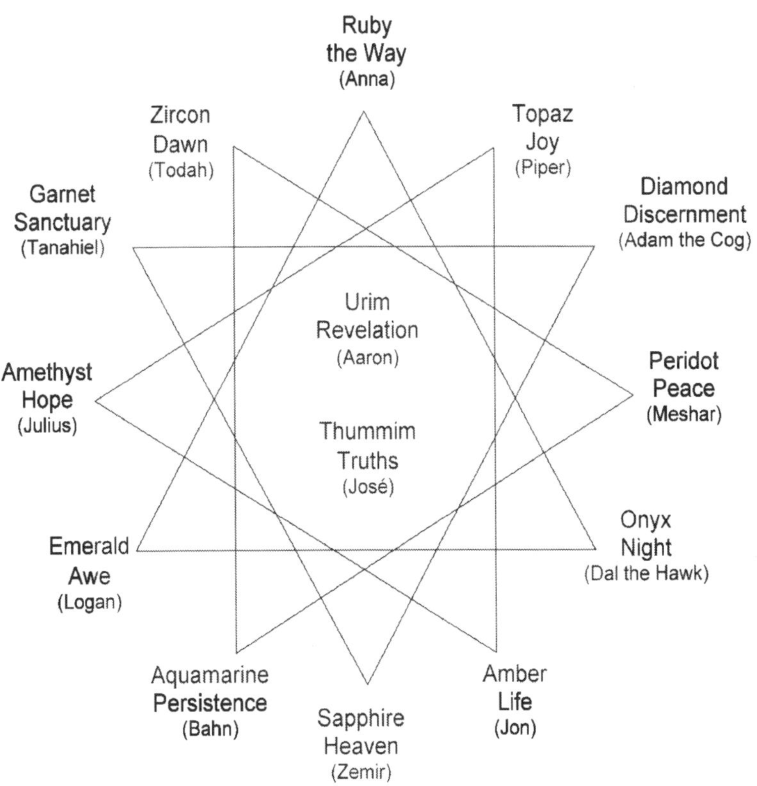

It had been nearly six months since the surprise visit by the Chancellor where he delivered his second request, and the creation of the humanoid neared completion. The Chancellor had offered him unlimited resources to bring this about, and Gideon and his team had worked tirelessly in shifts around the clock to accomplish it. A variety of technological hurdles needed to be overcome, but, when they had just about despaired at the enormity of the task, inspiration would strike one of them "out of the blue," and breakthrough would occur. They had so many patents pending that they had lost count. They had everything now from skin, to organs, although the eyes had been especially difficult, to all of the senses, and even emotions. This being could hardly be called artificial any longer. When they completed their work, he would be indistinguishable from a normal human being, except maybe in size and strength. He stood nearly ten feet tall and had the strength, speed, and stamina of a dozen men. His gideonite brain proved the key to the integration of all of his function. Dr. Anakim had used all the gideonite that remained in order to develop, fabricate, and program the brain, the masterpiece of the project. Tomorrow morning the Chancellor would be on hand for Ben's awakening. Adonis had named him Ben Ha-ChiyaRa, the son of Ha-ChiyaRa.

Under the cloak of darkness they moved Ben from the laboratory to a room in Adonis' residence. It resembled a typical bedroom, except they constructed everything oversized for the benefit of its occupant. Being ten feet tall had some drawbacks. Ben lay comfortably on his back in bed and appeared to simply be sleeping. Adonis, Baalel, and Gideon sat by his bedside while two members from Gideon's team, a couple who were both physicians and scientists, stood nearby.

Adonis spoke, "What are we to expect?"

Gideon replied, "From Ben's perspective it should be as simple as awakening from a good night's rest. We have given him a fairly extensive set of memories for the past year. He knows that he is your son, his mother was killed in the auto accident a year ago, and he is recovering from a head injury received in that accident. The trauma put him into a coma for nearly six months and has left him with partial amnesia. He doesn't remember anything before the accident. You can fill in the rest of the blanks as you desire."

Adonis nodded his approval, "Good."

Gideon continued, "While he has been unconscious we have been able to not only program his mind, but also to test much of his ability and sample many of his actions and reactions. He scores off the charts on just about anything we could throw at him. I think you will be very pleased."

Adonis nodded again. "Do we need your two assistants here for his awakening?" Gideon shook his head and dismissed them. They would be able to observe everything from the two-way mirror on the wall.

Gideon spoke again, "I have implanted a few hypnotic suggestions that are voice independent. I will give you a list of them, but this is the first one," to the being in the bed he commanded, "Ben Ha-ChiyaRa, wake up."

Ben's eyes opened and he looked at Adonis, "Father," he spoke in his huge bass voice as his eyes moved to Gideon, "Dr. Anakin… and I'm afraid I don't think I have met you," the last he spoke to Baalel.

"Ben, this is Baalel, my trusted friend," said his father.

"If you are my father's friend, then I am sure you will soon be mine also. I am pleased to meet you. What time is it? I seem to have slept in."

Adonis replied, "No, you're fine. Why don't you get dressed and meet us in the dining room."

"Yes, sir." He stretched as he sat up and swung his legs lithely over the side of the bed. Adonis, Gideon, and Baalel left and Ben dressed quickly in shorts, t-shirt, and khaki trousers. He preferred to go barefoot while in the house. He stopped quickly at the toilet, used the facilities, splashed some cold water on his face, and slicked back his long mane of hair. He looked like some barbarian god. Then he went to breakfast with his father, Gideon, and Baalel.

"Son, I hope you slept well?" Adonis asked.

"Yes, extremely well and dreamed too." Ben responded.

"Oh, and what did you dream about?" said Adonis.

"Mother was there and said I was on the edge of something momentous. I felt like it would be the coming together of all I was made for," Ben explained.

"All you were made for?" Adonis looked questioningly at Gideon.

"You know, father, all I have been trained and educated for, everything I have experienced, all leading up to and preparing me for my greatest challenge."

Adonis visibly relaxed. "Yes, son. I think that was more than a dream. Perhaps the foreshadowing of what is ahead." Their conversation drifted on to other things; the state of the economy, affairs of state, the plight of the church in its fight against the heresy of the dissidents. As they finished, Adonis thanked Gideon profusely for all that he had done and excused him. Gideon left, his greatest accomplishment completed.

After Gideon had gone, Adonis, Baalel, and Ben exited the dining room and headed down into the underground bunker. Ben seemed unfazed, as though he had been there before, until they came face to face with a luxuriously ornate door, covered in occult signs and symbols.

Ben stopped cold. "What is beyond that door, father?" He obviously thought he had never been beyond it, but then there would have been no way for Dr. Anakin to implant that information in his memory because Gideon had never been beyond it.

"Would you like to see?" his father responded.

Although Ben appeared in the full bloom of manhood, he acted overcome with childish expectation. "Yes," he said exuberantly.

"And so you shall," his father added. Baalel touched the door with his staff. It disappeared, and they walked down into the cold and near darkness. They entered the chamber with its stone altar and sacred bowl. Baalel drew a knife from beneath his robe. Before you could blink, Ben had disarmed him. Adonis quickly responded, "It's OK, Ben. He means no harm. Give him back the knife, please." Ben reversed his grip on the blade, looked at it with surprise, and handed it back to Baalel. Baalel sliced the palm of his own hand, squeezed a few drops of blood into the bowl, spit in it, muttered a few unintelligible words, and touched it with his staff. There came a sudden flash, a muffled concussion, and the room became lightly smoke filled.

As the smoke cleared, it revealed a being of shimmering light, flanked by two dark angels. Both Adonis and Baalel dropped to their knees. Ben did not. Ketseph and Yahrey both drew their dark swords, but Ben's eyes remained fixed on those of the being of light. They handed their swords to the Luminescent One, and he brought them together. Another flash of light and, this time, a seeming implosion. What remained in the being's hand defied description.

The voice of searing darkness said, "Only Ishbibenob ever wielded a weapon such as this, and with it he would have slain king David of old, had it not been for the intervention of another." With it laying across the palms of his two hands he extended it to Ben. "With this weapon the children of the virgin will not be able to withstand you!"

As Ben took it from his hands, the three beings disappeared. Ben then lifted it to his mouth and seemed to swallow the weapon. He turned around to face his father and Baalel. "There is something missing," he said, "I am incomplete." He paused for a moment as surprise and awe registered across his face. "Mary!

Where is Mary?" It sounded like a command and no one spoke like that to Baalel, let alone Adonis.

Adonis regained his feet, astonished at what had just transpired. "Mary was killed when my warriors destroyed the farm where she was staying.

Ben cocked his head to one side, "No! She is still alive!"

As they returned from the bunker, his father explained that Mary had been the wife of one of the leaders of the dissidents, that she had died of a brain aneurysm and been brought back to life by Dr. Anakim. She had been the first use of the new material known as gideonite. That same material had been used to restore him, Ben, after the terrible auto accident that had claimed the life of his mother. Because they both shared gideonite in their brains, there must be some link between them. Mary had been given back to her husband in hopes that she would betray the location of the entire group of dissidents and, while she had not, his Triparteum warriors had discovered it and destroyed it, with her, he thought.

"No. She is alive," Ben restated, "but I am unsure of her location. It is currently hidden from me."

PART 10

WAR

Chapter 32 - Exposure

And he will reveal himself as an angel of light. His word will confuse and confound, so that (if it were possible) even the elect would be led astray.

from the "Chronicles of the Apocalypse"

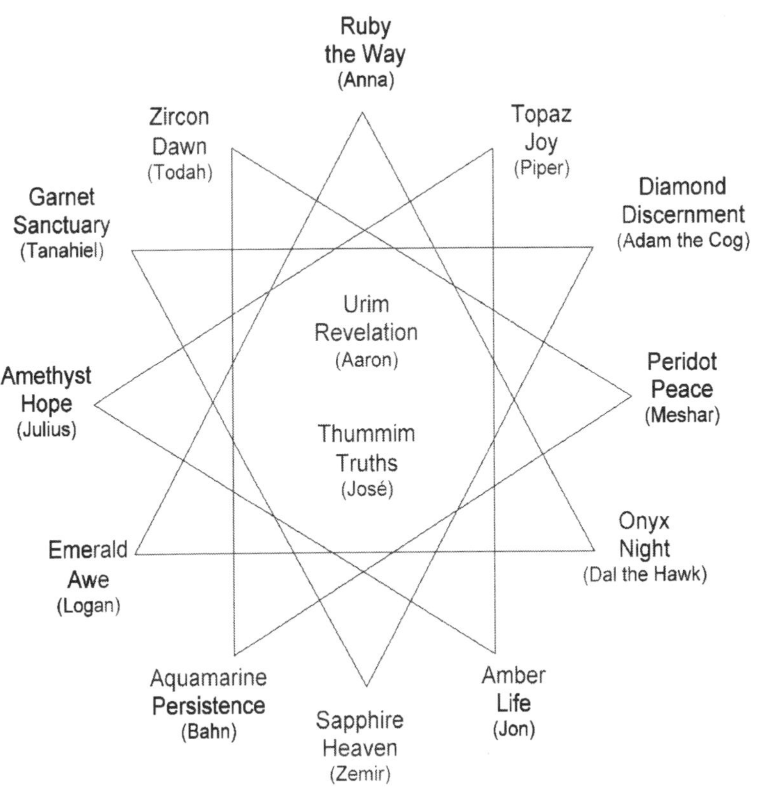

The time had come for the delivery of Julius and Judy's baby. They believed that it would be a boy, at least Aaron had prophesied the birth of a boy. They would have a son, they would name him Hashadiel and he would be instrumental in bringing many to the Sanctuary during the world's most desperate times. Judy had gone into labor. She walked the confines of their small cottage as long she could. Her water had broken about an hour ago. Their friends and neighbors prayed. Bahn and a midwife waited nearby. It seemed that Bahn's tribal lore included the delivery of children. Olga, one of their near neighbors had trained as a midwife before she and her husband Sven had found the Sanctuary. More and more people showed up, just one or two at a time as something or someone led them to the tunnel. Julius, Judy, and their troupe had been the only large group this past year. The emotional and spiritual atmosphere remained one of awe and wonder as everyone worked, served, and worshipped together. It seemed like Eden had been restored except, instead of the Tree of Life at the center of everything, the pillar of Fire burned, God's physical manifestation in their midst.

The contractions came now hard, regular, fast, and close together. Bahn and Olga confined Judy to her bed. The intense labor only took a few short hours, but to Julius it seemed a lifetime. Then, he had a son. Newly cleaned, wrapped in cloths and having successfully nursed, Julius picked him up and carried him outside. He wanted Judy to rest and delighted to present his son to the village. Everyone greeted him with joyful oohs and aahs as he exited the cottage and announced to the awaiting vigil, "It's a boy, just as Aaron prophesied!" He walked slowly among the crowd of friends and neighbors as they viewed another miracle of God's life in their midst. "This is Hashadiel, but I will not formally name him until his circumcision and the ceremony of his dedication next week." He smiled. There would be additional joy tonight as they gathered for their evening communal meal. The news was sure to spread quickly.

Sadness tempered one person's joy. After giving Julius her smiling congratulations, Mary turned and left the cottages, walked past the cooking and eating areas, and into the forest. Despair and sadness overwhelmed her for she remained barren. She had never been able to give Jon a child and although the pain of that fact had been left long ago in the past, now it rose its ugly head full force. Her eyes filled with tears and she continued to wander until she found herself in the tunnel that connected the Sanctuary to the rest of the world. She wandered without thought to where she went, even in the near darkness, until she haltingly emerged into a brilliant sunlit day on the other side. She followed the stream a little further and then sat on a rock, seemingly coming to her senses as she turned back towards the opening of the cave.

Suddenly she felt a faint concussion of wind and a small tremor of the ground. She turned around, and there he stood in all his magnificent splendor, ten feet tall, bathed in the sunlight, with the sculptured countenance of an angel. The artificial wings with which he flew folded up behind him. He smiled and her heart fluttered.

"Mary," he said lovingly, I can give you what your heart so longingly desires. I can give you a son." Her heart nearly stopped.

"Who are you, sir?" she questioned.

"I have many names. I am Ben, the Son of the Great One, the image of he who was, was not, and yet lives again." His voice was like honey to her soul. "And what is this place?" He gestured towards the cave.

She stammered, "This is the Sanctuary, our place of refuge."

Ben replied, "Go and return with your husband. I will remain here, anxiously awaiting your return." Mary turned and did as he asked.

She found Jon walking in the corn fields, one of his favorite tasks.

"Jon!" she exclaimed, "the most wonderful thing has happened." She continued to explain about her attending Judy's labor, the birth of the baby boy, and her following sadness, despair, and how amidst her wandering she found herself outside the tunnel, the entrance to the Sanctuary, where she met an angel of indescribable beauty. "He told me that he could give us a son and that I was to come back here, fetch you, and return to him." She could hardly contain her joy. For some reason this didn't seem to "ring true" to Jon.

"Why didn't he just come in here with you to meet me?" he questioned.

A bit exasperated she responded, "I don't know, I'm just telling you what happened."

Jon countered, "Did he say I must return with you alone?"

"No," she replied, a bit more crestfallen. "I just sensed that was his implication."

"And how did you find your way through the tunnel in the dark?" he asked.

"I don't know, I just did! Come on Jon, he's waiting for us!" She feared she might lose her miracle.

"I want to ask Aaron and Alathos first."

Her bubble completely burst. "What if he doesn't wait for us?"

"He said he would, didn't he?"

"Yes."

"Then he will."

They met Aaron and Alathos returning from the pillar of fire. They often met God there while ministering before the Ark. Mary's hope returned as she retold the story to the both of them, even amidst Jon's questions. The peace that the two of them always seemed to radiate and their encouraging nods as she spoke, rekindled her hope and strengthened her conviction to return to the angel.

"I have only a single question, Mary," responded Alathos. "Who should return with you and Jon. Let's return to the Pillar of Fire for just a moment."

Chapter 33 - Explosion

And the Image of the Beast will make war on the children of the Virgin. He will consume them with flame from his lips.

from the "Chronicles of the Apocalypse"

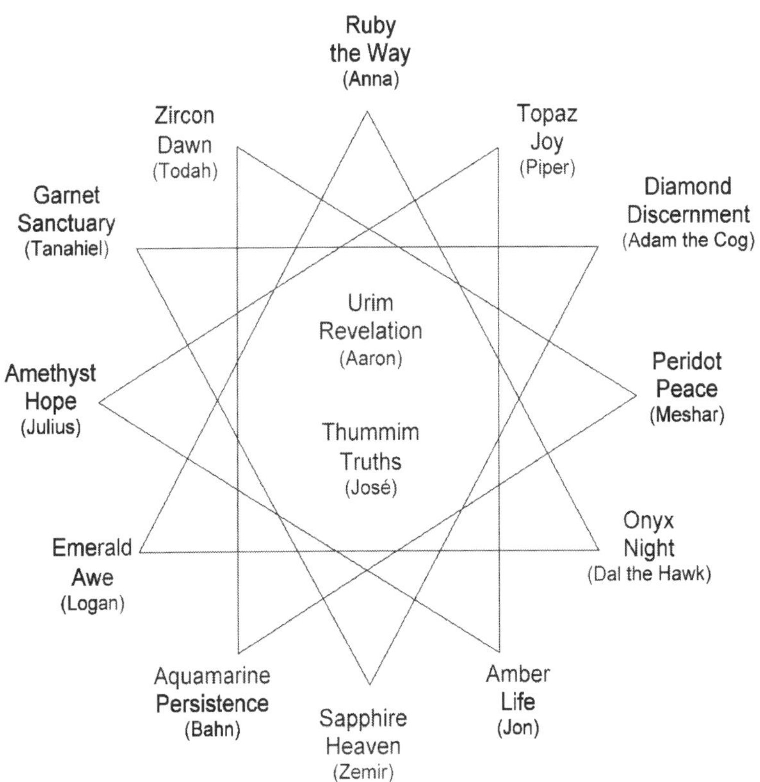

As the four of them, Jon and Mary, Aaron and Alathos, returned to the pillar of fire, anther group met them. The angel Teedhar flanked the group on the left side and to his right stood Julius, Logan with the hawk Dal perched on his shoulder, Anna and her angel Zek. Mary began to share her story when Julius stopped them.

He said, “Yes, we know. We have been asked to join you and complete one final exploit for this season. We are to go meet the angel Ben Ha-ChiyaRa, although he is not really an angel. He is the son of Adonis, the Chancellor of the Triparteum and wields a weapon of immeasurable power.”

“And what are we to do when we confront him?” asked Alathos.

Julius answered gravely, “As you can expect, we will know when the time comes.” They all turned. Alathos invited Anna to ride on his back. The angels, Mary and Jon, Julius and Aaron, and Logan with the hawk followed them. Together they headed for the Sanctuary’s exit.

When they reached the mouth of the cave, they fanned out into a semi-circle and then Mary and Jon stepped forth.

“I have brought Jon as you requested,” Mary’s voice quivered.

“I did not ask that anyone else accompany you,” Ben replied sternly.

Anna spoke, “You did not forbid it either and it seemed prudent.”

Ben sneered at Alathos, "A centaur! Is this the Alathos of legend? I pictured you more imposing."

"Looks are often deceiving," Alathos replied.

Ben's sneer remained as he said, "And a dwarf with a bird, is this a circus?" he continued. "Two angels, against whom I am more than a match. The rest of you are of no consequence at all."

The hawk launched himself into the sky and Ben opened his mouth and unleashed an explosion of catastrophic proportions. At that very same moment, Teedhar stepped forward, broke Mary and Jon's hand hold and pulled Jon behind him. The concussion threw everybody back into the cave except for Mary and the angel, whom the blast incinerated. The ceiling of the cave then collapsed, burying the others, fire burned abound the mouth of the cave.

Chapter 34 - Epilogue

Yet this is not the end, but only the beginning of birth pains of what is to come.

from the "Chronicles of the Apocalypse"

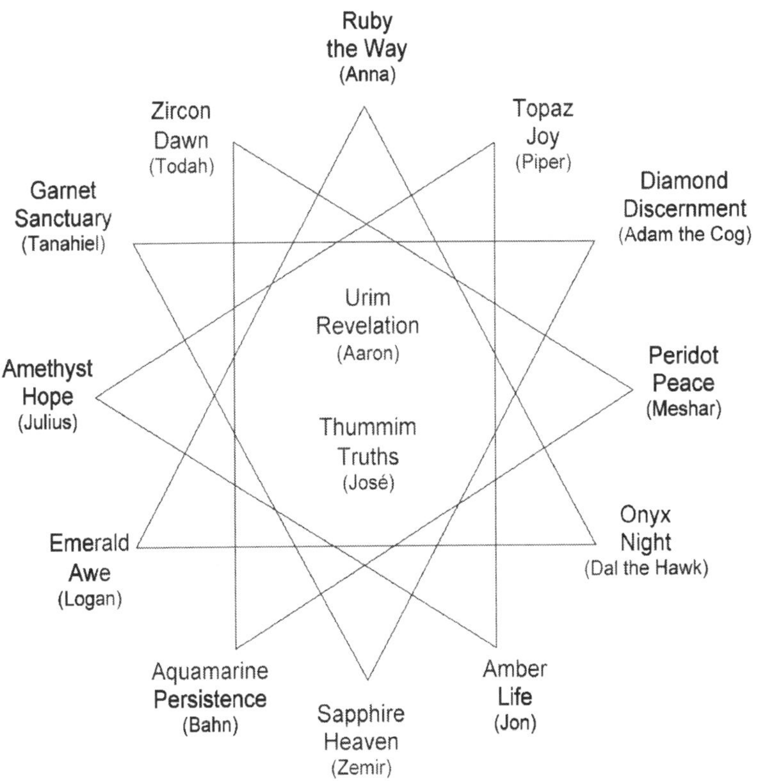

Ben flew to a nearby hill and stood with his feet firmly planted on the small outcropping that overlooked the dying flames. As he watched the mopping up operation below, he exclaimed, "In the name of my father, it is finished! I trapped them like the rats that they were, a cancerous disease eating up our perfect people, our superior race, the new mankind. Like a skillful surgeon, I removed the cancerous growth and purged our people clean again." Stepping off the rock and picking up his canteen, he poured a handful of water ceremonially into his hands and washed his hands over and over again. A demonically victorious smile slowly grew upon his face. "Ah, the sweet taste of triumph," he whispered to himself. As he watched the Triparteum forces continue to sift through the charred rubble below. He saw a sudden flash of steel, a reflection like that of a small hand mirror up in the hills, caught in his peripheral vision. He quickly focused his enlargers, bringing the area into an intense magnification. "Nothing, it was nothing," he thought. He continued scanning the area to quiet his still-nagging doubts. Then he saw it, high in the sky, something circling.

He touched the transmitter at his throat. "Kouta, is that one of our drones?" he said pointing. Kouta drew the projectile weapon to his shoulder, quickly checked through its scope. Ben heard the sharp crack of its report. Ben kept his enlarger trained upon the object, a bird. Suddenly in mid-flight it fluttered, spasmed, and fell like a rock into the trees.

“That should be the last of them,” reported Kouta.

The smile returned, “Good job, Kouta,” he intoned touching the transmitter again. Then as he released the pressure upon his throat. He said silently to himself, “The Chancellor, my father, will reward me well for today’s work.”

The bird came falling out of the sky directly overhead. The old man had heard the weapon’s report. The dead bird kept falling. An instant before it smashed into the ground, its large wings extended fully open to stop its headlong descent to death. Still, he landed with a terrific jolt. Before the bird, kneeling at the stream, was a strong boned, old man with a sleeping child strapped almost carelessly to his back. Even having just climbed the hill, the old man was not breathing heavily, he seemed hardly winded at all. Dal lifted his head and slowly stretched his wings testing them.

He hopped closer to the man and said in a whisper, “Which way now, my brother?”

The man turned smiling in his graying beard. “The others know that a second witness is needed. From here we must go forward. This is no time to retreat. While we seem to have lost the battle, the eventual victory will be ours.”

The bird nodded in agreement and together they moved forward, into the dense forest.

Glossary of Names as Introduced

Chapter

1. Ha-Geen - Eden's crippled gardener
   Zebo - a gazelle in Eden
   Chayeem - the Tree in the middle of the garden
   Urim - the stone of Lights-Revelation
2. Hal - archangel and choirmaster of heaven
   Clay - the first man
   Dawn - the first woman
   Kate - the pelican
   Zemir - an angel, Kate's friend
   Tummim - the stone of Truths
3. The Awe stone - Chayeem's seed transformed
4. Hail'yk - R'gel's lost sword
   Alathos - the centaur
   Son of Chayeem - sprouted from the seed of Chayeem
   Bigtha - apprentice gardener
   Hashamayeem & Meshar - swords made from Hail'yk
5. Jon - Bahn's pupil
   Bahn - the woodsman
   Ringmaster - head of the circus
   the stone of Life
   the stone of Persistence
6. Anna - a young girl
   Zek - Anna's guardian angel
   Mr. Clown (Julius) - the humorous illusionist
7. Julius - the humorist, amateur magician, clown
   Rex- the bully
   Maximus - the circus magician with the Hope stone
8. Logan - the dwarf, animal whisperer, Awe stone finder
9. José - The Saint, itinerant preacher, priest
   Jackknife (Todd) - pool player
   Judy - Jackknife's sister, druggie
   Adrian - José's dog
   Rev. Jim Click - hospital chaplain
   Christine Andrews - hospital nurse
10. Bruno & Natalia - trapeze artists
    Mary - Jon's wife
    Juan Carlos & Maria - farm workers

11. (Mary)
12. Piper - homeless girl, pipe player. finder of the Joy stone
13. Aaron Elias - the prophet
    Ed - another pool player
14. The Triparteum - one world's government
    Adonis Ashereem - Triparteum's chancellor
    Tri-World Church - Triparteum's recognized religion
15. Gomed Akkub - Triparteum soldier
16. Meshar - Gomed's new name, given the stone of Peace
17. Dr. Gideon Anakim - Nobel prize winning scientist
    discoverer of Lucidium & Gideonite
    Adrian Quick - Director of the Science Board
    Quicksilver - personal ID, GPS, and finance biochip
18. -
19. -
20. Ark of the Covenant - an ancient Old Testament artifact
21. Ayah & Anan - angelic protectors of the Ark
22. Tanahiel - another young woman
    the Eagle - bringer of the Sanctuary stone
23. Todah - a plain young woman
    Teedhar- Todah's guardian angel, bringer of the Dawn stone
24. Adam - the cat-dog clone (Cog), Discernment stone
25. Dal (Defiance) - the hawk, finder of the Night stone
26. -
27. Caleb - the dog next-door
28. Hashadiel - Julius & Judy's son
29. -
30. Baalel - Adonis' personal prophet and medium
31. Ben Ha-Chiya-Ra - humanoid son of Adonis
    Keteeph & Yahrey - two dark angels
32. -
33. -
34. Kouta - Ben's general

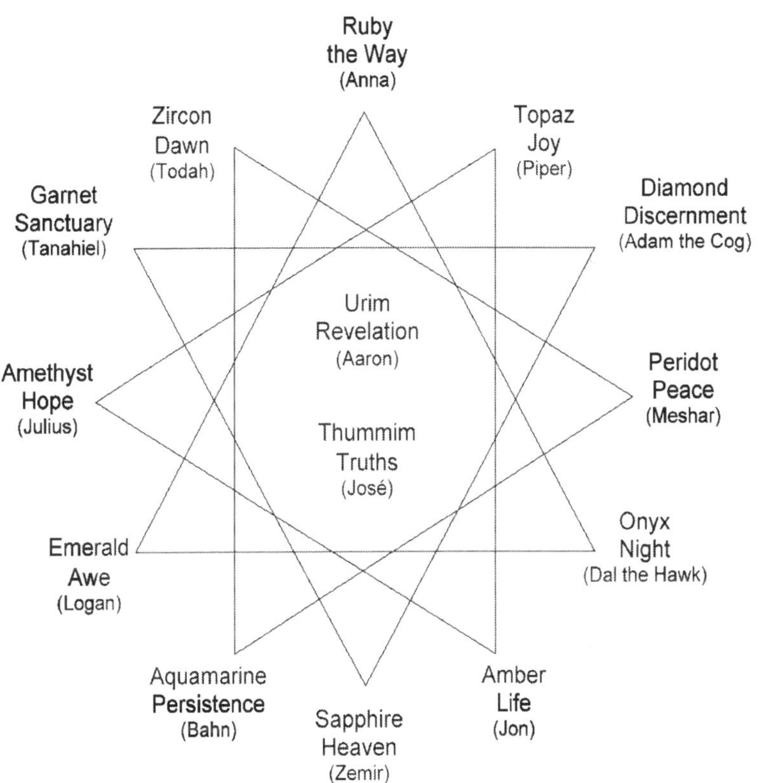

Ruby
the Way
(Anna)
Topaz
Joy
(Piper)
Diamond
Discernment
(Adam the Cog)
Peridot
Peace
(Meshar)
Onyx
Night
(Dal the Hawk)
Amber
Life
(Jon)
Sapphire
Heaven
(Zemir)
Aquamarine
Persistence
(Bahn)
Emerald
Awe
(Logan)
Amethyst
Hope
(Julius)
Garnet
Sanctuary
(Tanahiel)
Zircon
Dawn
(Todah)
Urim
Revelation
(Aaron)
Thummim
Truths
(José)

Out of the Sanctuary

(the Sequel)

Chapter 1 - Is This Hell?

And they said to him, "What is your riddle, Let us hear it."

And he said to them, "Out of the eater came something to eat.
Out of the strong came something sweet."

Judges 14:14

Darkness, so very dark. Julius held his hand up in front of his face, but could not see it. The explosion, if that is what it had been, had deafened him and he still could not hear anything. He thought the entrance to the cave had collapsed, but he was unsure. "Maybe I am dead and this is hell. I am alone and in utter darkness," he thought. Then someone bumped into him. Zek cautiously stood and drew his sword. Suddenly he saw light, not flaming sword light, but a translucent glow from the sword, giving off enough light for them all to see for a few cubits around them. Aaron stood. Alathos had given him a crystal, had fashioned a setting for it, and attached it to the top of Aaron's staff. It gave off a light bluish glow of its own. Anna had been thrown from Alathos' back by the concussion of the explosion, but miraculously onto the only patch of grass nearby. She got to her knees.

Alathos regained his footing and addressed her, "Anna, can you see what happened?"

In an almost prayer-like attitude she responded from her knees, "The false angel, Ben, spoke and used the sound of his voice as a weapon against us. Mary and Teedhar were destroyed in the blast, but the rest of us were thrown back far enough into the cave that when the entrance collapsed we were essentially unharmed."

Alathos probed further, "Anything else?"

She continued, "It seems as though they think we all died in the collapse. They have retreated triumphantly."

Jon had been staggering to his feet when he heard Anna mention Mary's destruction. He collapsed back to his knees,

"Mary is dead, again? She can't be. How can you be certain? You no longer wear the Way stone," he cried.

"I'm sorry Jon, but it's true. She perished in the blast with Teedhar," she spoke just above a whisper. "God gave me this sight when He gave me the Way stone. When I gave the stone back to Him he let me keep His gift. I'm so sorry, but she's gone."

Jon began to weep uncontrollably. This time he had not lost her to the aneurysm, he had lost her to the enemy. Little Logan stepped from behind a rock. They had almost forgotten that he and the hawk Dal had also been with them. He placed his hand on the kneeling Jon and emitted the sound of shared pain like the whimpering of a hurt animal. Then he embraced Jon and his embrace seemed to suck all the grief out of Jon's heart. Jon abruptly quit crying. He looked up at Logan and, as the beginnings of a smile began to grace his lips, leaned in and kissed him lightly on the forehead.

"Thank you Logan, I needed that," was all he said.

Logan turned his attention to Anna, "Dal took wing just before the explosion. Did he escape?"

Anna dipped her head again, "Yes, he did. They tried to shoot him out of the sky and they think that they did, but he was only pretending to be hit. I lost sight of him as he fell into the trees, but I believe that he is alright." Zek had handed his sword to Jon and lifted Anna onto Alathos' back again.

Aaron turned to face Alathos, "What will we do now? The Triparteum has destroyed the entrance to the Sanctuary," he said with obvious concern.

Alathos smiled, "And what makes you think this was the only way in and out of the Sanctuary?"

About the Author

William (Bill) Siems

Bill has always been a storyteller. His wife says he still tends to share the truth creatively with a mind that processes in live action and living color. He grew up in south Seattle and has lived in Tacoma since 1972.

Initially working in hospitals, Bill joined the Boeing Airplane Company in 1979 as an Industrial Engineer and taught Employee and Leadership Development the last 15 years of his 32 year career. As a teacher, trainer and facilitator, Bill would often develop and teach his own material. He has written numerous short stories and dramas, but this marks his first published novel, and it appears it will require a sequel to complete the story.

Retired since 2011, Bill spends his time mentoring, teaching, acting in community theater, and enjoying his family. Bill and his wife of nearly 50 years, Nancy, live near their three children and six grandchildren.

If you can't find him at home in his office, he is probably across the street playing with the neighbor's dog.

Made in the USA
San Bernardino, CA
23 December 2018